# MURDER
## ON SKID ROW

# MURDER
## ON SKID ROW

Charlene Wexler

authorHOUSE®

*AuthorHouse™*
*1663 Liberty Drive*
*Bloomington, IN 47403*
*www.authorhouse.com*
*Phone: 1-800-839-8640*

*First published by AuthorHouse      1/12/2010*

*ISBN: 978-1-4490-7358-9 (e)*
*ISBN: 978-1-4490-7356-5 (sc)*
*ISBN: 978-1-4490-7355-8 (hc)*

*Library of Congress Control Number: 2010900258*

*Printed in the United States of America*
*Bloomington, Indiana*

*This book is printed on acid-free paper.*

This book is dedicated to the three dentists in my life;

# Sam, Mike, and Lew.

# PROLOGUE, 1966

THE AGED BUILDING'S WINDOWPANE RATTLED as it was bombarded by hollowing spring wind and rain. I stood motionless, staring out at an empty Madison Street. My mind concentrating on the two druggists who were recently murdered, was startled by a voice behind me, "Doc."

I jumped at least two feet at the sudden interruption to my thoughts.

"Boy, you are tense!" the voice continued.

I swirled around to face thick black eyebrows surrounding hard, sharp eyes on a medium-built, middle-aged Caucasian male.

"Sorry, do you have an appointment?" I asked.

He dropped the *Chicago Tribune* on my desk. "What do you know about the murders?"

I stared at the paper on my desk. In bold print the headline on the April 1, 1967, *Chicago Tribune* said, "Double Murder on Skid Row." Finally, I looked back at the man standing before me.

"Who are you?" I asked.

He grinned at me. "Sorry, I didn't introduce myself. I'm Detective Anthony Scarianno," he said as he opened a worn brown billfold and showed me his identification. "Mind if I sit down?" he asked as he lit a Chesterfield cigarette and pulled up a chair next to my desk.

Puzzled by his appearance in my dental office, I answered, "I've already talked to the police."

He took a deep drag on his cigarette before looking up. "My job is to dig deeper than the police."

Sitting down at my desk, I looked up into his face "The front page of the *Tribune* called it botched robberies. I would have to agree with them. This area is loaded with drug addicts needing money."

"Come on, Doc. Two botched robberies about a month apart. There's something wrong with this scene," he answered as he put his cigarette out in my dental assistant's ashtray and continued with a nonstop account of the murders.

"There are two employees at the registers, two or three customers in the store when a tall, thin black teenager with a baseball cap pulled down low mumbles a name. One employee, the guy, goes to the back of the drugstore. A pharmacist comes to the front of the store, and he is shot point blank, and everyone in the store lets the shooter disappear on a bus, and of course no one knows who he was! The truth is on this street, and it is my job to find out why they were killed."

The tone and volume of his voice gained momentum with every word. I could hardly concentrate on what he was saying. I felt compelled to answer with something.

"In this neighborhood, no one wants to get involved. They're afraid to snitch!"

"What do you know, Doc?"

"More, now that you've told me the details."

He smiled at me and took a minute before commenting. "Hey, Doc, you're learning how to survive here."

Detective Scarianno continued, "Okay, Doc, once, but the same scene occurs again one month later. I think everyone around here knows who shot the druggists, and who hired him."

He took out another cigarette and offered me one. "Do you smoke, Doc?"

I hesitated. My fingers twitched, my eyes followed the smoke rising up toward the ceiling, and my mind kept saying yes, but the words out of my mouth were, "No thank you. I'm trying to quit because my fiancée hates me smoking."

"I once had one of those, a wife too. Don't give in, or they'll change everything about you."

He lit his cigarette, took a deep drag, blew the smoke to the side, and then looked directly into my face.

"How well did you know Abe?'

"Not very well. He was my landlord," I quickly answered.

"Then how come you never sent him a rent check?"

"I had free rent for a year." For some reason my voice was trembling. "I don't like your questions. Do I need a lawyer?" I asked.

"You tell me! Were you one of the doctors taking kick-backs for scripts?" Turning around and putting the palm of his hand up to my face, he mumbled, "Don't answer. That's not my department."

He got up, stamped his cigarette out in the ashtray, and walked around the office while I stood up and silently watched him. He stood by the operatory and picked up the drill. Turning toward me with a grin on his face, he said, "The only thing that ever scared me as a kid was a trip to the dentist!" Walking on, he stopped next to my antique dental cabinet. "Nice piece of furniture!"

I stood up and walked over near the cabinet; lessening my guard, I explained that the tall mahogany 1890 cabinet was a major find.

While I was concentrating on the cabinet, he surprised me with a question. "Did you hire someone to kill Abe and Dave?

My hands and my voice trembled as I looked up to face him. "What?" I asked

"Was Abe holding out money on you?"

"I don't know what you are talking about," I answered with mounting resentment.

"The police found the gun in an alley. It belonged to Abe Meyer and was stolen about three months ago, when the drugstore and your office were broken into. The guy was shot point blank with his own gun. From informers on the street the police are narrowing in on the shooter, a young black kid. We believe he was hired by someone, and it's my job to find out who that was."

I regained my composure. I said, "Listen, I am not playing any games. I'm only twenty-four; I graduated from dental school last May, opened this office in August hoping to help the downtrodden, and as far as I'm concerned, this interview is over."

The detective picked up his coat and cigarettes, dropped his card on my desk, and headed toward the door.

"If you think you can help, call. And Doc, stay around, don't go on any vacations."

Halfway out the door the detective turned around. "Why did a nice young kid like you open up a dental office on Chicago's Skid Row neighborhood?"

# CHAPTER 1

I STOOD IN THE MIDDLE of the office, recalling when my father asked me the same question only nine months ago.

My father was helping me carry the last of my dental equipment up two flights of dark, broken, dirty stairs to a dilapidated fifty-year-old terra cotta and red brick building located only a few miles from Chicago's loop and my alma mater, the University of Illinois Dental School. It was a hot, humid day in August 1966. Twenty-three, young, and excited about opening my first dental office, I may have been pushing my dad too hard, because he was huffing and puffing as we twisted around the narrow stairway leading up to the second floor and my office.

Anxious for him to see the improvements I'd completed in the office, I quickly opened the door and flicked on the light switch, only to be disappointed by his reaction.

"You're crazy putting good money into this dump," he said as he looked down at my new dark blue patterned carpet and the freshly painted walls. "I'll never understand why you're opening your first dental office on Chicago's Skid Row."

"Dad, it's not like we come from a neighborhood of castles. You taught me to take care of people from all walks of life, and these people need care too." It was August 1966. I was fresh out of dental school, very idealistic, and very poor.

1

"Anyway, the owners of the drugstore on the first floor of the building are giving me a year's free rent."

"Didn't I teach you there's no such thing as free rent? What do they want in exchange?"

"My only obligation is to send all my prescription patients to the pharmacy."

"I still don't like it. Your patients around here are drunks and addicts. That's different than working poor people. I'm worried about your safety."

"You're worried, Dad? You were the one who introduced me to this West Side area. As a boy I went with you to Maxwell Street for our Sunday bargain hunts. We noshed on hotdogs from the stands. Though what really enchanted me were the stories you told about growing up there among the peddlers, shop owners, and the Jewish and Italian gangs."

"I had no choice, Mel, we were poor, and it was a different time. As an immigrant I had to be tough to survive."

"Believe me, I've had to be tough growing up on the South Side of Chicago, too," I said as I touched the scar near my eye. Even though I had a muscular build on my five-foot-nine frame, I had been no match for Dink McNairy that day back in high school when he called me "dirty Jew."

Changing the subject, Dad asked, "Mel, what are you going to do with this broken-down piece of furniture?" He slapped the side of it, inspecting the wood.

I had scavenged the area for old dental equipment, as the price of new equipment was out of my range. In the process, I had found an old wooden mahogany dental cabinet. It stood on legs and was almost six feet tall. Inside were medicaments and ivory-handled instruments. I couldn't wait to refinish it and use it to hold my dental instruments. My father thought I was crazy.

"Dad, look at the workmanship on this cabinet. You're always telling me that nothing is made like it used to be. It even has a secret locking drawer to hide money."

"You'll need it—if you make any money in this neighborhood," he answered as we pushed the cabinet out of the hallway and into my new office.

My dad had spent his whole life trying to find a way out of the old and into the new. My parents came here from Romania when they were children. My father was the oldest of eight. He worked his whole life peddling fruit and vegetables from a truck. He had to get up at two in the morning to get to the market. I was the first person in the extended family to go to college, and they were proud of the fact that I had become a dentist. I had fulfilled the American dream.

Finished, we sat down and rested before locking up.

I smiled as I looked around my office. It was small, about 250 square feet. The one window looked out over the drugstore facing Madison. *I must remember to buy an interesting shade for it, as that is the window my patients will be looking through,* I told myself. The lab for developing X-rays and working on models for dentures, crowns, and partials was too small. Maybe at a later date I would take some space from the waiting room and enlarge it.

"Mel, stop daydreaming. Let's go. I hate to leave the truck unguarded in this neighborhood."

I turned off the lights and locked the door. Dad and I headed down the steps and out to his ten-year-old red pickup truck. Skid Row looked pretty quiet as the sun was setting. The flophouses dished out beds on a first-come basis.

"Dad, let me take you out for dinner. I couldn't have moved everything without your help."

"Nah, Ma will have dinner at home. We can't do that to her."

My mom and dad were the perfect couple, married over fifty years, and still totally devoted to each other. They came from similar backgrounds and liked doing the same things—shopping, working and staying home. I worried about my fiancée, Cindy, and me. We loved each other, but we were at odds about so many things.

Dad gave a sigh of relief as we entered the truck and started for home. I guessed he was really worried about the truck being broken into. Inside his truck were all his tools and his memories of days in the South Water Market.

"Mel, I didn't mean to be rough on yeh. The office is starting to shape up. You did a good job on the painting."

"Those years of growing up, helping you paint, plumb, and fix everything in the house and on the cars were a real learning experience."

His face slowly broke out in a smile. "I remember when you first helped me paint the house. I made you go over that ceiling three times, and you were about to pound one on me."

"I was only about eleven or twelve. That demand for perfection did help me get through dental school."

He gave me a big smile, showing his new bridge. "You're a good son, and a great doctor. My teeth feel real good."

He was my patient throughout school, sitting in the chair for hours while my professors graded me. True, he had the time now that he was retired.

I SPENT THE NEXT WEEK installing equipment, cleaning windows, scrubbing floors, etc. My expenses were minimal, because my one-chair office, though vacant for years, was originally occupied by a dentist and was still plumbed for dental equipment. Through the grapevine I found an independent equipment man who helped with the installation of my chair, dental unit, and X-ray. Until I made some money, the waiting room would have to do with five card chairs, my mom's old end table, and a few paint-by-number pictures I had made years ago.

The large radiators in each room were no longer used, as the pharmacist had converted the medical offices along with the pharmacy to central heat. Air conditioning would have been nice, but at least there was cross ventilation with windows in each room. Most of the other occupied buildings on the street were still being warmed by radiators. This treat on Skid Row should help my business.

The undersized bathroom down the hall needed work. The pull-chain toilet had been converted to modern plumbing, but the concrete walls were cracked, the mosaic tile that at one time must have been beautiful was dirty, and discolored, and there was no running water in the marble sink. I would have to ask my landlord to do something about that. In its day the office building, with mahogany woodwork inside and terra cotta figurines outside, was probably one of the outstanding properties in the area. The hallway even had the remnants of a crystal light fixture. Built fifty years ago and neglected for the last thirty, time had taken its toll on the facility.

I spent several days going up and back to the drugstore to use their phone while waiting for the phone company to come out and install a telephone by my desk. Finally Abe, the pharmacist, asked what was wrong. When I told him, he pushed his glasses up the bridge of his nose and smiled from ear to ear. "They won't come out here unless you know someone. A phone is a good idea for protection, but believe me, you won't need it for appointments. I'll call for you, my boytshik."

As I was walking out of his pharmacy, he called to me, "They come in colors now. Should I get you a pink one?"

I looked back in his direction. "Standard black will be fine!" He had a different sense of humor. I recognized it as what my mother would call, "West Side Humor." The immigrant Jews, who grew up on Maxwell Street and Chicago's West Side, had their own way of dealing with life.

Three hours later I came back down to the drugstore to thank Abe. I had learned one of Chicago's political rules—clout gets the job down. With my phone installed, I was now ready to open my first dental office.

My dental office's opening celebration was very small, just my mom, dad, Cindy, my fiancée, and a few friends. It was hard to get many people to Madison Street in 1966. It was considered a neighborhood of bums, drunks, addicts, and lost souls. The streets were full of broken liquor and beer bottles and cigarette butts, plus needles and garbage. The buildings were broken down, with cracked windows and chipped paint. The only commercial businesses were pawnshops, a few restaurants, and the drugstore. Most residents lived in shelters, flophouses, tenement apartments, or on the street. The flophouses were sleazy, dirty places with rows of beds, closed windows, and usually one bathroom per floor. Inhabitants were consistently robbed of their meager belongings. Many welcomed a day in jail just to get a clean bed and a hot meal. Drug dealers, winos, and prostitutes were everywhere.

Men who had once held down jobs and had families were now unshaven, dirty, thin, and unrecognizable. They could be found fighting over nickels, dimes, and cigarette butts. These men and a few women came from all walks of life—rich, poor, white, black. Many were injured Vietnam War veterans unable to adjust to life back in the States. They lived off of disability insurance, while most of the others lived off of welfare. Their only motivation in life was to gain enough money to buy drugs or liquor.

"Spare any change?" was the language of Skid Row.

There was a tremendous shortage of medical personnel in the ghetto areas. To correct this, the state of Illinois, in the 1960s, voted to increase welfare payments to doctors, dentists, and pharmacists willing to work in these areas. Older medical personnel already in the areas were finally making some money. Younger medical graduates planned to work in the areas for a short time to earn enough money to pay off student loans, and to be able to afford the opening of nice offices in the suburbs with posh clientele. With this in mind, I opened my first office on Skid Row.

# CHAPTER 2

IT WAS MONDAY, SEPTEMBER 3, 1966. Advertising by dentists was frowned upon, so I put a very small sign in my window saying, "Open," and waited for my first patient. After several hours, a bedraggled, toothless soul came up the stairs.

"Hey man, are you one of those tooth pullers?" he asked.

Laughing, I answered, "I'm a dentist. My job is to help you keep your teeth. In fact, if you get in the chair, I can make you some." Taking out a patient card, I asked for his name.

"They call me Ace."

"Ace can't be your real name."

He grinned. "You right. That's been my name since I been a young man, pulling those aces out of my sleeves." He stopped a minute, probably reflecting on those far away days.

I started to lead him to my chair, but he jumped out of my grip.

"Put your stuff away, I'm not getting in no chair. Nobody's gonna pull my teeth no more!"

"Today, I'll give you free dental care," I countered. "Wouldn't you like to have some teeth to eat with?"

He answered, "No need to chew, I just drink."

"Okay," I said as I turned away from him and went back to my office.

He followed me and grabbed hold of my coat. "I have a good deal for yous. If you give me a pint of Italian Swiss for every patient I brings you, we can become partners."

Ace and I became partners. An hour later he came back with another toothless guy and a shopping cart loaded with stuff.

"Ace, you can't bring that shopping cart into my office. It takes up too much space. How did you get it up the stairs with all that stuff in it?" I queried.

"My belongings goes where I goes, lest they get stolen."

"Where do you get the shopping carts? The closest grocery store is about three miles away, and the drugstore doesn't have any carts."

His toothless mouth opened into a big smile. "You right. They hard to get, that's why I protect this one."

I looked at him in his long black overcoat. "Ace, why do you wear that thing in the middle of the summer?"

"It's gots pockets."

I had almost forgotten the patient Ace had brought into my office. He gave him a push toward me as he walked out. While carefully maneuvering his cart through the door, he yelled, "Give Berger some dentures. He young enough to need them. He don't talk much, shell shock from the war. I be back for him, and my wine money."

After he left, I understood why he wore the coat. My desk was missing my radio and packages of sugarless gum, but he left the Parker fountain pen set my dad had given me at graduation. I would soon learn that Ace could flick a billfold from a pocket faster than a squirrel could pluck a nut from a tree.

I turned to my patient, and I now realized not only could this auburn-haired, freckle-faced young man not speak, but he was also missing his left arm. Afraid that he couldn't understand me, I asked him for his identification using a mix of sign and verbal language. He clearly understood me and handed me his disability card. I was surprised to see that he was another patient who had the address of the drugstore as his home address. Later, I would learn that the drugstore worked as a post-office and currency exchange for the homeless bums to receive their welfare, Medicaid, and disability checks. After helping him into the chair, I took his glasses from him. They were nice frames, but one of the lenses was missing.

"Why don't you go down to the VA and get your glasses fixed?" I asked. His eyes followed me, but he didn't make any response to that, though when I said open wide, he did. Instead of pulling all his teeth, I was able to repair some with new fillings and fit him for a bridge. Whether he would come back for it was anyone's guess.

When Ace came back, I asked him to take Berger to the VA hospital for new glasses.

"No carfare," he answered

"Here's a dollar for carfare."

Phil, the physician who had an office next to mine, looked in and shook his head. "Bet you ten that money will never be used for carfare."

To my surprise, a few days later Ace brought Berger back for his bridge. This time Berger had glasses with two lenses.

I put my arm around Ace and thanked him. Then I called Phil into the office. Reluctantly, Phil parted with a ten. Ace straightened up and held out his hand for his part of the ten. "We partners, right?"

THE NEXT DAY, ABOUT AN hour after I opened my office, three dirty, raggedly dressed guys rushed through the waiting room and into my operatory. I was overjoyed—finally some patients!

"There's a guy out there with a knife, help us," they cried. It turned out they were hiding from a robber who was trying to take their meager belongings. I quickly closed the door and went for the phone to call the police.

As I picked up the phone, one of the men yelled, "Police won't come here. Get out your knife or nightstick."

"I don't have any."

"Use your drill."

"Help me push the chair against the door. That should do it," I answered.

I became alarmed when I heard loud hollering.

"No way am I giving up my bottle! Get out of here! I gots a knife too!"

Next, I heard the steps creaking as someone quickly ran down the steps.

One of the guys in the room with me said, "It's okay, open the door, Ape-Gravy's gone.

"You know the robber?" I questioned.

They looked at me funny as they all piled out. Opening the door, we found two guys sitting on the floor. One was holding up his bottle of Wild Irish Rose and the other one was holding up his shoeless feet.

"I outwitted him this time. He took my coat and shoes. My money's in my socks." My shoeless friend smiled, showing a toothless grin.

"I still have my baby," his friend said as he hugged a half-empty pint of Wild Irish Rose.

"While you're here, how about getting your teeth fixed?" I asked, thinking here was a golden opportunity to get patients.

Looking up at me, in unison they each asked, "How much you gonna give me if I lets you fix my teeth?"

Realizing this group was hopeless, I went back to cleaning up the office. As I was busy spraying freshener around the room Phil, the physician from down the hall, looked in.

"What are you doing?"

"This place always smells of alcohol, tobacco, dirt, and sweat."

He laughed, "You'll get used to it."

*I hope not*, I said to myself.

SLOWLY, I STARTED TO GET more patients. They came mainly from the pharmacy.

"Doc, Abe, the pharmacist, told me you can give me a script for pain in my tooth," was the common complaint. When I made the patients sit in the chair and get treatment, some became very agitated.

"No way am I getting in any chair. Don't you touch me with that thing!" they would answer, pointing to the drill. "You just give me the script and I takes it to the Doc downstairs."

Being young and naïve, I didn't realize the pharmacist was playing a prescription game. Two partners, Abe Meyer and Dave Miller, owned the drugstore. They had been in the area for many years. Meyer had grown up in the adjacent West Side area. They had watched Madison and Halsted Street deteriorate from poor immigrants to lost souls or Skid Row, as the rest of the city called the area.

They owned one of the few legitimate businesses still operating on the street. The people living in the neighborhood depended on Doc Meyer and Doc Miller for medicine, check cashing, credit, and advice. They were the "godfathers" of the neighborhood. Anyone connected with the area conducted business in their store. They were open seven days a week, devoting more time to the store than to their families.

Besides being there to help their customers, they plus several doctors in the area found a way to capitalize on the new state welfare system. The doctors wrote multiple prescriptions for each patient the pharmacy sent them. The patients brought the prescriptions to the drugstore and exchanged them for money, liquor, or tobacco. The pharmacist paid the doctor a percentage of the money he collected from the state off of the prescriptions. I was not willing to play the game and would probably be asked to leave at the end of my lease.

The druggists were very different. Dave, a man of few words, was tall, thin, and mild mannered. He wore a black hairpiece with a touch of gray. His clothes were nice-fitting designer wear. He always wore a white pharmacy coat over them. It was hard to judge his age. Though he was probably older than he looked, Dave kept a low profile, staying in the back filling prescriptions, and handling the paperwork. Every year he bought a new Cadillac, which was always parked out front, right behind the bus stop. His hours in the neighborhood were the store's hours. It was a job to him.

To Abe the store was his life. He was a short, stocky, bald man in his sixties, dressed in cheap clothes that were usually wrinkled and spotted. In his back pocket there was more often than not a police club. He drove a seven-year-old blue Oldsmobile that was normally filled with boxes. His loud baritone voice made up for his stature. Walking into the drugstore, one could always expect to hear Abe arguing and joking with the locals. Today was no different.

I went downstairs to complain to Abe about the prescription requests. Upon entering the store, I saw him walking from the back of the store toward the front and the liquor counter. I smiled as I watched him making his rounds, picking up papers and cans off the floor. His first stop was by an old bum dressed in tattered pants, who pleaded with him for a pint of wine.

"God damn it!" Abe bellowed. "You owe me an arm and a leg already."

"Come on, Doc, you know I'll pay when my welfare check comes. Just one more pint, Doc, I've got the shakes," Lucious said as he held out his trembling hands.

Abe angrily answered, "You drunken bum, get the hell out of here!"

Meanwhile, his face broke out in a grin as he slipped a pint of Wild Irish Rose to his customer and friend. Jackson, the employee standing behind the liquor counter, burst out laughing, while he held up a pad of paper with names of customers who received credit from Abe. "Abe, we never going to make no money that way!"

Abe continued maneuvering down the narrow aisles, which were stuffed to the gills with metal racks holding all kinds of merchandise. The place looked more like a cheap department and liquor store than a drugstore. He had everything from cans of food to costume jewelry. What he didn't have was a soda fountain, but most drugstores were eliminating them now.

In the toy section he picked up a cute little curly-haired baby girl, reached into his pocket, and produced a candy bar, which he handed to her. Turning to the child's mother, Abe said, "Vera, this one is getting bigger and cuter all the time. Soon she'll be stealing my candy like Gus, your older one."

He turned around and waved his hand at two bums standing in the doorway. In his loud, booming voice he yelled, "Hey, Dearborn, I heard you found two fins. Have Jesse fix you up with something special for them."

"Otis, don't stand in the doorway. Get your black ass in here. There's a bottle waiting for you."

Soon his arm was around me. "Mel, good to see you. How's business? Must be slow, I haven't gotten many scripts from your department."

Before I got a chance to answer or complain to him, two policemen entered the store, and Abe took off.

I turned to Sandra, his most trusted clerk, "Trouble." I said softly.

"No," she answered. "Those two are here for their cigarettes and bottles of Jack. Trouble left before you walked in."

"Who," I asked.

"Just old Roy, doing his usual cursing, and arguing."

"I haven't met him yet."

"You will."

Sandra handed me a coke. I thanked her. Abe was in the back by the pharmacy talking to the policemen, so I went back to my office.

By NOVEMBER, MY THIRD MONTH in the office, word spread that there was a new tooth doc that could alleviate pain and supply you with enough teeth to chew food and tobacco. As business increased I realized I needed an office girl.

Darlene answered the ad. She was a light-skinned, heavy, but neat -looking, pleasant speaking black girl, somewhere in her late teens. Her black hair was ironed straight, not in one of those new afro styles, and she had a nice smile, showing a mouth full of pearly white teeth.

"Are you still in high school?" I asked.

"Been out a year," she answered.

*Good*, I thought. *She'll be able to keep my hours.*

From my experience with other applicants, I didn't ask her to fill out the long application I had prepared. I was learning about the neighborhood.

"Darlene, have you had any experience in a dental or medical office? Can you add and subtract?" I asked.

"I worked at the free clinic down the street, and I come with a bonus for you."

"What's the bonus?" I asked cautiously.

"Tyrone, my boyfriend, will be your bodyguard."

"Why do I need a bodyguard?"

"Man, you a dumb white boy. Don't you know where you are?"

I whirled around to see this six-foot-three black as coal hulk towering over my slim five-foot- nine frame. My first thought was, *He could be a Bear's tackle.* My self appointed guard had a jacket on with the name Black Rangers, which meant he was a member of one of the major gangs in the area.

"You're both hired," I answered. Better to have them on my side.

With a big smile Tyrone gave me a hand slap. "Smart dude! How about a five-dollar advance on my pay?"

I opened my billfold and took out a five-dollar bill. I had been warned by Phil that I would be hit for protection money. I didn't like the idea, but when in Rome …

Tyrone was the type of employee who came and went according to his discretion, but he spread the word that I was an accepted member of the neighborhood, so I could now be assured that my car radio, hubcaps, and battery would be there at the end of the day, and that my office would no longer have broken door locks and smashed windows.

A FEW WEEKS LATER, DRIVING around the corner to the front of my building, I parked my five-year-old, cream-colored Volkswagen Bug next to a new black Lincoln Towncar. Leaving my car, I walked around the Lincoln, concentrating on all the features of the new 1968 model, almost tripping on someone lying on the street next to the car. I jumped.

"What are you doing?" I asked the teenage black boy working on the rear wheel.

"Hey, Doc, not your business, less you want to buy the car. I can sell you it real cheap after I empty the wheel." He shook his head and continued his task at removing the wheel.

Looking down, I realized that Spider, one of Tyrone's friends, was removing the whole wheel from the car.

Deciding this was not something I wanted to get involved with, I ignored him and started to walk toward my office. On the way I stopped by Leo, who was opening the iron gates to his pawnshop. Leo and I had connected. He was about ten years older than I was—slim build on a five-foot-eight frame, small eyes covered by black-rimmed glasses, originally from the South Side, a Hyde Park High School graduate, who, like me, enjoyed repairing and building things. Actually Leo sort of had a Woody Allen kind of look and personality.

"What are they doing?" I asked him.

"You don't know?"

I shook my head.

Leo looked around before moving in toward me and in a muffled voice, he answered, "They steal cars and transfer drugs to each other in the wheels. The car may be worth about three thousand, while the wheel could have twenty-five thousand dollars worth of drugs inside."

"Why here?"

"We're right off the expressway," Leo explained matter-of-factly, pushing his horn-rimmed glasses closer to the bridge of his nose.

"What about the police?" I asked. Leo gave me that look I was getting from everyone on the street when I asked a question that showed my innocence.

On my way to my office, I glanced at all the stop-and-go traffic on the corner and the activity in the vacant lots. I finally understood what was happening and why there were so many young teenagers around a block without family buildings. I would learn over time that there was an occasional raid and some poor, dumb user would be put in jail while the provider of the drugs took his profits and went scot free.

Upon entering my office, I took a good look at Tyrone's arms. Just a few months ago when I first hired him, I was still too naïve to notice the puncture marks on his arms. I thought about how things in the United States had changed in a few short years. In the 1950s and early 1960s when I grew up, the drug scene hadn't surfaced with the white middle class. Then the Vietnam War brought protests, hippies, and drugs everywhere. From 1962 to 1966, my dental school years helped keep me unaware. I had no time for anything but study. I now realized the Camelot that died with President Kennedy's assassination, never existed in neighborhoods like this one.

I wanted to know more about the people in the neighborhood. Tyrone was sitting near Darlene doing nothing but smoking a cigarette, so I started with him.

"Tyrone, do you have any brothers or sisters?" I pulled up a chair close to Tyrone.

Tyrone stared at me with suspicion before answering, "The Rangers are my brothers."

"No, I mean blood siblings."

His eyes narrowed, and his lips pursed, "Sure, my mama, she got a bunch of kids running around somewhere. My dad, if he still be alive, probably does too."

"Where do you live? There are no residential buildings on this street."

"Projects." Tyrone's answers were now down to one word.

"Aren't they over a mile away? Why do you and your friends hang out here?"

"Safer here," he answered with a smirk.

Phil, the physician who was busy eating my morning donuts, looked up. "Don't you mean fewer cops, around, close to the expressway for deals, and the weak bums make easy marks?"

"Fuck off, you fat pig."

Tyrone got up, grabbed Phil's packet of Camel cigarettes out of his hand, and walked out the door.

"Why do you put up with that scum?" Phil asked as he walked out, cigarette in one hand and donut in another.

Though I didn't answer, I knew the main reason was I was afraid to ask Tyrone to leave.

I walked down the hall to the toilet, thinking about all the new characters I was meeting. Hearing voices, I looked out the small, dingy toilet window to the alley. I recognized Tyrone and Spider, and I wondered what they were up to now. Tyrone stood in the dim light of dusk against a wall in the alley counting money, when Spider sidled along beside him, pulled out a switch blade from his jean's pocket, held it up near Tyrone's face, and grabbed the money. "Give it back," I heard Tyrone yell.

Spider pushed the knife away, and held up the money. "Six dollars. You dumb nigger. Did you rob some poor old blackie? When you gonna learn, the money's with the whitey. No wonder you can't get anywhere with the Rangers. You big, but you ain't nothing but a big pussy." Spider put on his black sunglasses, tossed the money at Tyrone's feet, and walked away. Tyrone stood there angry and frustrated. I watched the smaller figure of Spider leave the alley. When he was barely in sight, Tyrone yelled, "Hey, Mother fucker, don't you ever talk to me like that again!"

I moved away from the window. Spider was right. I had heard Tyrone complain that the Rangers didn't give him no jobs. A shiver went up my spine as I left the toilet and walked back to my office. These two were dangerous. Spider was cool, confident, and smart, while Tyrone, despite his huge size, was dumb, and easily maneuvered by Spider. Tyrone reminded me of the bully on the south side who picked on those smaller and helpless just to feel important.

Phil was standing in his doorway. "Watch out for Tyrone. Remember, he's a crack addict."

# Chapter 3

I DECIDED TO TREAT MYSELF to some modern dental equipment. The new contour dental chairs being used in sit-down dentistry were the rage, but I couldn't afford them. I found a company that sold add-ons to old chairs. The light blue addition made my 1940s chair look as good as new. I tried sit-down dentistry and found it very difficult. My one-chair operatory was too small for a dental assistant, and I had been trained in stand-up dentistry.

Anyway, Darlene could never be a dental assistant. She was good with the patients, but her knowledge of dental equipment and procedures was nil.

As I walked into the operatory after lunch, I detected a familiar odor.

"Darlene, this place smells like a restaurant," I said, exasperated. "What's going on?"

"Oh, I'm just cooking a chicken."

"Cooking a chicken! In what?"

"The autoclave. It does a great job."

"You're kidding, a chicken in my brand new autoclave! Are you crazy! An autoclave is used to sterilize instruments!"

She backed away, frightened at my outburst. "Nobody told me."

I realized if she did work in the clinic, she learned very little beyond making appointments and collecting money.

"Okay, Darlene, you're right, nobody told you. From now on we will have a class on dental procedures every morning."

Surprisingly, she caught on better than I expected, memorizing the names and identity of the instruments and the procedures. To help her feel like a real dental assistant, I bought her a white uniform, which she wore every day. Darlene's favorite procedure was helping me take impressions for dentures.

Making dentures was big business in the sixties before the advent of implants. Most of my patients were missing teeth because they never took care of them.

Gregory, a big, heavy-set guy with streaks of gray showing through his brown hair, probably in his fifties, dropped about four sets of dentures on my desk.

"I cleaned my car out and found these. None of them ever fit. Do you want to buy them?"

"No, but I can try to make you another pair."

I thought about my grandmother's teeth always sitting in a glass of water. On welfare where the state was paying, Gregory tried again. He had a tough ridge and very little patience, so I understood his problem with dentures. Considering that at some point he had all his teeth pulled, there were no alternatives.

A few weeks later when he left the office with his new dentures he seemed satisfied, and I was happy until one day, months later, Darlene told me, "Gregory needs a new denture. He lost them in his car again."

I didn't believe it until one day when I saw Gregory's car. It was loaded with clothes, blankets, food, a bicycle, a toaster, papers, garbage bags, cigarettes, ashes, etc. It was his home, making him one of the wealthiest bums in the area.

I walked into the office laughing. Tyrone asked, "What got your goat, doc?"

"I just saw Gregory's car. It's parked on the vacant lot next to a big old Ford."

Tyrone's eyes opened wide. "Stay away from that lot, and that Ford."

"Why? I asked.

"Doc, I'm your body guard, and I'm looking out for your safety."

He was right. A day later the police were busy towing the Ford. The word on the street was the trunk contained a body burned so badly that it was impossible to identify it. I left my office early that day, and the whole way driving home I thought about how close I had been to the dead body.

When I arrived home in my safe South Chicago neighborhood, I glanced around suddenly, noticing the trim gardens with colorful flowers, girls jumping rope out front, and boys playing softball in the alleys. I walked around to the backyard, giving my mom a kiss while she was taking down laundry from the lines. She had a washer and dryer, but she still liked to hang the clothes outside if the day was nice. While growing up here, I never thought about how other people lived. What an awakening Skid Row had become. I checked the paper for days, but there was nothing about a burned body, and nobody on Madison Street seemed to know anything about it. I was finding out, besides, *spare any change, I don't know nothing*, was also the language of Skid Row, and the ghetto.

As WINTER APPROACHED, MOST OF my patients and my helpers seemed to be lacking coats, so I rounded up old coats and boots from family and friends and dispersed them, which turned out to be a blessing, since 1967 was one of our snowiest winters. Instead of just grabbing the things out of the boxes, the homeless spent time picking out and trying on the clothes. Jim was so pleased with an old plaid scarf that had been my uncle's, and Otis pranced around in a pair of red boots, even though he was told they were girl's boots, and Gregory loaded his car with everything that was not taken. I got in the habit of leaving clothes in a box outside of my office.

Phil told me I was crazy. "Mel, they are only going to sell your stuff for drugs, or wine money."

I answered him, "If just one guy keeps the clothes and stays warm, it's worth it."

WHEN I LEFT MY HOUSE one Thursday late in January it was cold, but the sun was shining through the clouds. The weather report on my car radio was for light snow. By two o'clock the snow was coming down heavier and thicker than the weather had predicted, so I closed up my office and went down to my car. Looking around, I realized I should have left earlier; most businesses were closed, and my VW was buried under the snowfall. After clearing the snow off of my car, I started out, only to discover the roads hadn't been cleared yet, and I was driving through blizzard conditions, with very limited visibility. It took me forty minutes to go a mile, so I abandoned the car on Halsted, along with the rest of the ditched cars stuck in snow banks, and I started to walk. The stores were closed, and the streets were deserted except for a small black-and-white shaggy dog hiding in the doorway of the Greek grocery store. He looked so wet, scared, and hungry, that if I'd had my car I probably would have taken him with me. I dug into my pocket and tossed him a cracker, the only food I had.

From the looks of things, I guessed my chances to make it home were slim, so I changed my destination to the dental school, about two miles away. Trudging through the blizzard, I could hardly breathe. The blowing snow and gusting wind was strong enough to knock me over. It was the first time I had a clue of what it might feel like to be homeless and afraid. I was cold, tired, and not sure if I would find food, shelter, and a place to sleep. With luck on my side, I finally made it to Polk and Wood Street, and the entrance to the dental school.

There was a tall, muscular young guard at the door. Only people with some connection to the University of Illinois were let in; others were directed to County Hospital. A former teacher vouched for me, since I no longer carried any University of Illinois identification. Shaking the snow off of me like a dog after a winter walk, I entered the first-floor lobby, sat down long enough to catch my breath, and assessed my situation. My face, hair, and coat were soaking wet, but the rest of me was just tired. The student guard came over to me. "Doctor, if you are planning to spend the night here, I suggest you reserve a dental chair in the clinic. We're getting full."

At that point I realized there was no way to make it home that day. On the second-floor clinic I found familiar faces of doctors and teachers. Following the guard's suggestion, I staked out one of the new contour dental chairs as my bed for the night and then went to the third floor, looking for something to eat. The vending machines were empty, so dinner for me and my stranded companions consisted of shared pocket candy and gum. One teacher, who I promised to keep anonymous, produced a bottle of Jack Daniels. This helped us forget about the perilous weather outside. Funny, a year ago I was a student in awe of the three teachers, who were now my buddies.

Contacting loved ones was difficult. Besides the line at the one payphone, many circuits were down. I was able to talk to my folks Thursday night, but I couldn't reach my fiancée, Cindy, until Friday morning. Thankfully they were all fine. It took Cindy and another teacher five hours to drive the ten miles from their school to their home.

Friday morning the streets were no better. Some twenty-three inches of snow covered the city, and most places were still closed. The only public transportation moving was the elevated trains. Anxious to get home, I took the train near the dental school south to sixty-third and Stony Island. I then joined a group of people walking down the streets, through the mounds of snow, and around the deserted cars. Kids, outside throwing snowballs, and making snowmen, were enjoying their days off of school. People were out sharing food with each other and with the stranded walkers.

After about two miles of trudging through the snow, a trailer truck driver stopped. Operating one of the few types of vehicles able to drive through the streets, he was kind enough to give me and another walker a ride to within three blocks of our home. When I walked through my front door and smelled the aroma of my mom's home cooking, I gave a sigh of relief and collapsed onto my mom's sofa. After eating a delicious, hot chicken dinner, I slept for ten hours.

By Monday morning Chicago was back to normal, with cleared streets and milder temperatures, so I returned to my office. I stopped at the drugstore before going upstairs. Abe was in the back of the store. "Abe, thanks for calling my house on Friday."

"I worry about my friends. I looked for you on Thursday. I was going to take you with me."

"How did you get home, Abe?"

"Alderman Johnson got me home. Smart move on your part, to go to the dental school," he said while giving me a pat on the shoulder. "This was one of the worst storms I've ever been through. We lost a lot of customers. That jerk in the flophouse turned guys away. Many of the bums were found dead or severely frostbitten this weekend. Otis was one of them. He froze to death in a mound of snow on the empty lot next to our building. I'll miss him. He's been around here for years. I could tell you a dozen Otis stories."

A faraway look crossed Abe's face, and I instantly knew I would get one of his stories. "One winter, years ago when we were both young, Otis, strung out on something, came in here stark naked and asked for a pack of cigarettes. Afraid to say anything to him, I put the pack on the counter and asked for twenty-nine cents. When he went to reach into his pocket for money he woke out of his trance, looked down at his unclothed body, and ran out of the store. The temperature had to be in the teens."

Abe smiled and turned toward the pharmacy office. "See you later. Dave's not coming in today. I've got work to do."

I left the drugstore and walked upstairs. I wondered if Otis was wearing the red boots when he was found frozen. The building was quiet. Phil never showed up, and Darlene came in three hours late. I only saw two patients all day, so it would have been a good idea to take another day off, but I really wanted to pick up my car. It was still on Halsted, under a pile of snow, only now it had a ticket on the windshield. I was angry. Maybe I could get Abe to get Johnson to help me with the ticket. I guess I was lucky it wasn't towed to the pound.

# CHAPTER 4

BESIDES MY PATIENTS, I HAD my regulars who hung around the office hoping to make a few dollars by doing errands or supplying me with new patients. One of my favorite regulars was waiting for me when I opened my office one cold February morning.

"Hey, Doc, I brought you some coffee. You better stay alert so you won't get sued," Jim Bones said as one hand gave me coffee and the other hand was stuck out waiting for a few quarters. He genuinely intrigued me. Here was an intelligent, blue-eyed, blond-haired man living day to day on the street using every penny he could panhandle for drugs. His body was wasting away from the addiction. Most of the time his speech was slow, deliberate, and hard to understand, but today he was sharp, and we were having an intelligent conversation about the Vietnam War and the increasing protest rallies against it.

"Thanks, Jim," I said as I handed him a dollar and took a sip of the hot coffee which was in a cup from Miranda's Café. It probably cost him twenty cents. He was smart enough to bring me good merchandise. Sy, another one of my regulars, tried to charge me for my own coffee, bringing it to me in one of my cups from my lab.

"Doc, did you hear what happened over there at the end of January? Those God damn Viet Cong blew up our embassy in Saigon. President Johnson better get us out of there before we lose all our young men. There is no way we are going to win. In America we aren't trained for guerrilla warfare. Can't tell one from the other, can't tell one from the other, can't tell one from the other.

"Jim, were you in Vietnam?"

He looked up at me, grinned and for a moment he became Jim again.

"Yeah, I and many of my buddies on the street defended Voltaire's best of all possible worlds. Berger, he lost an arm and his voice box there."

"I thought he was born deaf."

"No, he was born whole, got shot up over there, and now nobody wants him. We were in the same platoon. Now we are in the same flophouse."

"Were you injured, Jim?"

"They say I was lucky because I came out whole."

"Did you go to college before 'Nam?"

He looked at me strangely and started to walk away while repeating over and over again, "Yeah, I'm whole. Yeah, I'm whole."

I watched him go, thinking, *what a shame*. Maybe all the protestors knew what they were talking about. Why, even CBS's news anchor, Walter Cronkite, bellowed out, "What the hell is going on over there?" Besides being disabled, most of the Vietnam War veterans on this street became hooked on drugs while overseas. The vets from other earlier wars were alcoholics, not junkies.

Any conversation that led to identity was soon aborted. I had thought Jim was too old to be in the Vietnam War. The Skid Row inhabitants had so worn down their bodies with abuse that a twenty-year-old looked like an old man. Everyone had a nickname; in fact, I was never called Dr. Greenberg, just Doc, like all other workers in any medical field in the area.

I was surprised to see Jim Bones at my door two days later—but I did give him an extra dollar the other day for the hot coffee.

As he staggered over to my dental chair and literally fell down on it I ran to his aid.

"What's wrong? I asked as I looked at his ashen face. "Should I call for an ambulance?"

"The dragon lady is bleeding," he answered weakly as he rolled up his sleeve.

I stared at his arm. Yes, right through her mouth the dragon lady tattoo on his arm was bleeding profusely. I quickly applied a tourniquet to his arm. With the bleeding under control, I went toward the phone.

With his other hand he grabbed my arm. "Please no hospital, just a bandage."

I tried, but there was no way to persuade him to tell me what happened, or to take him to County Hospital, so I treated him the best I could.

I took off his shirt, washed off his arm with an antiseptic, bandaged it, and gave him some antibiotics, coffee, and a donut. Putting the chair back, I told him, "I have no patients for a while, just rest."

I understood his reluctance to go to County Hospital's emergency room, where he would be waiting for hours to be treated. I wasn't sure, but I guessed he was in a fight over some merchandise. About two hours later he walked out of the operatory like nothing happened and started in on a normal Jim conversation.

"Doc, I want to ask you something. Were you in the army?"

"No, Jim, I'm 4F, a broken eardrum." I reached for his arm. "How's your wound?"

Ignoring my question, he laughed.

"What's so funny?"

"A broken eardrum and you became a dentist with that damn drill going all day." He shook his head. "The only thing funnier would be if your mama had a candy store."

Thinking about his quote from Voltaire the other day, and other times when he quoted Shakespeare or discussed his theory on Kennedy's assassination, I tried to help him get off the street.

"Jim, you don't belong here. You obviously spent some time in college. Where's your family? Let me help you get off the drugs and the street."

"My family's here, Doc, and I need the drugs to stay mad."

"Why are you so angry?"

"Not angry, Doc, mad, like crazy. Don't you realize only the mad can survive in this world? I appreciate the jobs, the medical care, the extra dollars, and the conversation, as long as you stay away from the lectures and the questions," he said, as he quickly took off. I felt frustrated as I watched him leave, probably, because I could identify with him easier than with the others.

# CHAPTER 5

SY, A NERVOUS LITTLE GUY, stayed around for days and then disappeared for weeks. He was actually very handy at fixing things when he was sober. He helped me install a small black and white television in my waiting room. It turned out to be bad idea. My waiting room became crowded with people who hadn't seen a TV in years. They walked up and back, changing the dial, thus causing fights over what they would watch, dropped garbage all over the room, and never thought of getting their teeth checked. I had hoped it would bring in a better class of clients from the surrounding neighborhoods. Sy was the only patient I got from the TV try, and he was getting work done free.

"Hey, Doc, can you put a star in that gold crown you're making for me?" Sy asked.

"What are you talking about?" I asked.

"Ain't you seen Tiger? He has diamonds on his gold crowns. He can do that because he got money from his girls."

Sy had just alerted me to a growing trend in the ghetto. Status was achieved through tattoos on your body and by the number of fancy gold crowns glimmering from your mouth. Once I started doing these crowns, my business increased tremendously.

Tiger even brought in his girls. Tiger was a typical pimp. He was thin, about almost six feet tall, very sharply dressed in a tailored black suit, purple shirt opened at the neck, and shiny black leather wing-tipped shoes. Most of the bums hanging around the building coveted those shoes.

He pulled up in a black Lincoln, and three girls emerged. As I looked over at my Volkswagen Bug parked next to his car, I thought that I might be in the wrong business. The girls, dressed in short skirts, skimpy beaded tops, and tons of makeup, ran up the stairs and headed straight to the crown cutouts. They then stood around the cabinet picking out cutouts as if they were picking out jewelry. Tiger, with his cold, calculating eyes, stayed in the background dangling a cigarette in his hand, while Sy tried to get anything he could for setting up the meeting.

"Mel, I want a half moon and a star," said one of the women.

"Millie, you only need one crown. Pick out one or the other," I said

"Aw, Mel, gimme two. My customers like them, and Tiger is paying. I'll give you a freebee."

"Millie, get in the chair and let's look at your teeth." Even though she was dolled up with face paint and bleached blond hair, Millie couldn't be any older than a young teen. I wanted to ask her how she ended here, but we were under the watchful eyes and ears of Tiger. Millie reminded me of my thirteen-year-old cousin.

Nicki, with flaming red hair and black fishnet stockings, wanted me to crown all her teeth before she was to have a nose job. One of her customers had broken her nose, and her face was a mess.

"You're kind of cute, with that dimple on your right side, your sandy colored hair, and tight ass. I would enjoy showing you a good time, Doc," she said, flirtingly.

I felt myself blush as I turned away from her, while trying to concentrate on my job. My goal was to teach patients how to save their teeth, not to want decay so they could get crowns with fancy facings. I quickly went into a lecture on dental health. As I was concentrating on demonstrating proper brushing, Tiger moved over to my chair.

"Knock it off Doc. Just finish up. The girls need to get back on the street."

When they left I stood staring at the wad of bills Tiger had handed me. My hands felt dirty holding them.

Nicki, one of Tiger's girls, in jeans, sneakers, and no makeup, greeted me at the door very early the next morning. Standing behind her was a cute little curly-haired boy, who couldn't be more than four years old. She looked around cautiously. "Doc, can you do me a favor?" Pulling the child out so I could see him, she said, "This is my son Tony. He fell down and knocked out his front tooth." Then she said to Tony, who was trying to hide, "Open your mouth for the doctor." The poor kid's mouth was all bloody where he must have been hit, I assumed.

I took his hand and said, "Come on, Tony, get in my big chair, and I'll give you a ride before looking at your tooth."

Tony followed me. After putting him in the dental chair, I moved it up and down a few times to give him a ride. I then took care of the wound, telling his mother to take him to the physician. "He lost a baby tooth and will have to wait a few years before the permanent tooth comes, but his lip may need stitches," I told her.

"No money, and no time. Tiger will be looking for me, and I have to get Tony back to my mother."

"Wait," I said as I walked next door and pulled Phil into the office. "No donuts today, unless you help me with this kid."

Tony's eyes brightened, and he talked for the first time. "Can I have donuts too?"

"If you stay still while we fix that lip."

Phil and I fixed Tony and sent him off with two donuts.

On their way out, I told Nicki, "I think I could find you a job where you could stay home nights with your kid."

"Thanks, Doc, but it won't pay as much, and once you're in this business, you can't get out."

By my sixth month on the street I was acquainted with most of the prostitutes in the area. This didn't sit well with Cindy. On a Saturday afternoon as we exited the car on the way up to my office, she asked, "Mel, why is that street walker blowing you kisses?"

"Oh, that's Millie, one of my patients."

I began to realize that bringing Cindy around to see the improvements I had made in the office was a bad idea, especially since she was decked out in an expensive blue knit outfit and gold jewelry, so I quickly showed her the office and escorted her back to the car. Once on our way, Cindy asked, "Isn't it time for you to get out of this neighborhood?"

Looking straight ahead while driving north on Halsted, I tried to tell Cindy how I felt about my Skid Row office. "It's hard to explain, but the people living here have become my friends. They just have had hard breaks in life. I know you want me to open up in the suburbs, but it takes a lot of money to open a suburban office, and I'm not sure I would get along with the North Shore crowd."

"Mel, you know my folks are willing to help you open a suburban office."

Cindy just didn't understand. She came from an upper middle class suburban family and didn't have a clue about not having enough money. She seldom ventured out of her neighborhood surroundings, and any place south of downtown Chicago was like a foreign country to her.

As was our custom, we went out every Saturday night, come rain or shine, mainly in the north suburbs or downtown Chicago. This Saturday we were meeting Cindy's friends Gary and Gail at the new in restaurant, Michele's, which was located in Lincoln Park, a neighborhood a few miles north of my office. The Lincoln Park neighborhood was doing a fast change from a crime-ridden area to a young people's hang-out. Old Town, just south, with its coffee houses, restaurants, and fudge shops was the "in" place to be.

Approaching Michele's, I found a parking space two blocks away on Clark Street. Cindy wasn't happy walking in the cold, windy night, but she kept quiet about it.

The restaurant, small and cozy, with wooden tables and petite flower vases on them, was located in a store front on Clark Street. Gary, dressed in bell-bottomed pants and sporting long hair, was carrying a small bag. Hoping I wasn't missing someone's birthday, I asked him, "What's in the bag?"

"A bottle of Mateusz . The charm of the restaurant is that you are allowed to bring your own bottle."

"Wine," I said, "is for the bums. I would rather have a nice stiff Jack and coke."

Cindy gave me a disapproving stare. "Mel, wine is the rage now."

With a sneer on my face, I answered, "Yes, Cindy, wine is the rage!"

As the waitress poured the red wine, I almost fell over at the prices on the menu, like seven dollars for a steak. I finally found something for four dollars, but I didn't know what it was. I thought everything in this restaurant was written in French.

"Cindy, what's this?"

"Coq au Vin."

"I can read it. I'm asking you what's in it."

The waiter came over. "Chicken, in wine, sir."

Cindy gave me another disapproving stare. "What's wrong with you?"

Gary added his two cents to the conversation. "Maybe you need to get out of that neighborhood. Gail and I would love to have you be our dentist, but we're afraid to go to Madison Street."

"Thanks, Gary. Now Cindy will be back on my case, to close the office."

For the rest of the evening, we made polite conversation as we ate and drank. Gary and I split the bill, and the four of us left the restaurant.

They waited for the bell man to get their new Chevy Impala while Cindy and I hurried down the block to my old cream-colored VW in its free parking space. Cindy made it clear to me that the evening was strained by my attitude.

"Mel, I can't believe how rude you were this evening," she said as she walked ahead of me with her hands folded against her chest.

I kept quiet. I guess the fact that Millie, one of the prostitutes I had treated the previous week, had been stabbed that day and it was unknown whether she would make it through the night, didn't help my disposition.

Most of the occupants of Lincoln Park were not aware of its new status. They walked down Clark Street and Wells Street looking at the vacant lots, the old, shabby buildings, and the taverns, instead of the newly opened antique stores, the restaurants, like The Steak Joint, and the folk song houses, like The Earl of Old Town. Close to the car a shabbily dressed man in torn pants, sloppy long-sleeve shirt, bloodshot eyes, no coat, and dragging a garbage bag full of his possessions approached us.

"Change for food, please," he asked as he held out a quivering hand.

I shook my head and continued on. Cindy stopped and dug into her purse. The bum's triumphant grin quickly turned to despair as she handed him several pieces of paper.

"What's this?" the guy asked, holding up the paper.

"I had these made special. It's a restaurant not far from here where you can get a good meal."

The bum handed them back to her. "You're crazy, lady."

She looked bewildered. "I thought he was hungry. Actually I bought several from Manny's Delicatessen for you to give out to your patients."

I looked at my petite, cute, thin fiancée in her expensive blue cashmere knit suit, Gucci purse, manicured hands, and coiffed hair handing out coupons to the bums. She didn't get it, but she was adorable.

"Yes, honey, this guy and most of my patients are hungry for alcohol or drugs." I then softened as I thought back seven months to my first days in the office, when I purchased bagels and cream cheese to give out to my starving patients. At least she hadn't given out coupons to Michele's, where I had just spent a week's worth of profit. We left the bewildered man and hurried down the street, got into my car, and headed north on the outer drive. Neither one of us talked much, though she did comment again about how I should open an office on the North Side or how I should be more involved in the wedding plans.

After kissing Cindy goodnight at her door in Northbrook, I got back into my car and started on the long drive home. While driving, I thought about how difficult it would be to have a dental practice with all Garys. Gary had spent the evening complaining about the service and the food at the restaurant. Even though I couldn't admit it to Cindy, I realized that besides the small investment my practice on Skid Row cost me, it gave me a chance to gain confidence and develop my own techniques. Some of my friends had enlisted in the army to get practice in treating patients before opening their own offices.

When I turned into the Dan Ryan I shifted my concentration to the road. I glanced at my gas gage and realized that it was close to empty. On Fifty-fifth Street I was lucky to find a Martin Station that was still open at midnight. Rain had begun during my drive and was now pounding the pavement, so the attendant reluctantly came out of the station. After he filled my twenty-gallon tank, I paid him his six dollars and told him to forget about checking my oil or washing my windows at this late hour and in the inclement weather. He was grateful to bypass the usual service required.

By the time I drove down Jeffery Boulevard, turned onto my street, and walked into my house, it was past two am. The house still lingered with the delicious smells of my mother's cooking and baking. I quietly entered the kitchen and noshed on some of her freshly baked strudel. I was going to miss Mom's cooking. I wasn't sure if Cindy could even boil water. Every occasion I spent with her family, we met at Peppercorns, Myron and Phil's, or Fritzel's Restaurant. I never had a home-cooked meal in her parents' house. Cindy and I were so different, yet I did love her.

# CHAPTER 6

IT WAS MONDAY, AND THE work week came around quickly. After spending an hour driving through traffic, I pulled into a parking space in front of my office. I exited the car, stopped to give Lucious's begging hand some change, and crossed the street, where I entered Miranda's Café. I sat down next to Leo, at one of the red-and-white checked tables.

Miranda's small gingham-curtained restaurant with her band of regulars had become my morning hang out. There was Tony Cheng, who owned the Chinese restaurant, rumored to have the best junk for those who could afford it; Charlie, who ran the flophouse, only suited for rodents; Leo, the pawnshop owner, who seldom asked where your merchandise came from; Phil, the physician, who wrote prescriptions for anything and at three hundred pounds ate everything Miranda could make; Abe, from the pharmacy; and Clancy, who drove the neighborhood squad car. Clancy and six of his ten kids had become nonpaying patients. He was another Tyrone, only he had a uniform. He and his rookie cop partner, Keith, never even left Miranda a tip for their daily free breakfast.

Miranda appeared with coffee pot in hand.

"The usual?" she asked me.

"No, I think I'll have pancakes this morning. Where's your daughter, Maddy?"

"That girl never showed up today. Down in Mississippi where I come from that would never happen. Why, my mama would have boxed my ears if I ever pulled that stunt."

"You're from the South? When did you come to Chicago?" I asked.

"I come up here in the early fifties. I had this job in Mississippi for this white family. I be the best damn cook in the whole county. Nobody made black-eyed peas, chicken and dumplings, pecan pie better than me."

"Why did you leave?" I asked.

"Down South they still treating us like there was no Civil War. I got nuff of yes ma'am, yes sir."

"Hey girl, stop that gabbering, and get me some of that good cooking."

Miranda quickly turned around. With a big broad smile on her face, she ran over and gave a white-bearded, coal-black, slow-walking old man a great big hug.

"Rufus, honey, when you all come back?"

Now I knew for sure why she reminded me of Aunt Jemima. Besides her outfit, a large, flowered, floor-length muumuu on her very full body and a matching bandana on her straight, black-haired head, she was once a cook in the Deep South. This made sense because her pancakes, grits, and cornbread were to dream about.

She came back to the table with plates of ten-inch round buttermilk pancakes stacked four high, dripping with butter and syrup. Putting the plates down, she leaned over and asked me, "Hey baby, when's your wedding?"

"Call me Doc, like everyone else. My wedding isn't until June 20. Why do you want to know?" I asked.

She grinned as she brushed her hand through my hair. "You still a baby in this neighborhood, wet behind the ears." Then she got serious, stood up, and looked me in the eye.

"Why do I want to know? Numbers, policy, honey. We tried your birthday. Maybe we'll have more luck with your wedding. Let's see, we got four-twelve-thirteen for Mel and six-twenty-sixty-eight for the date. Give me a couple of dollars and we can play partners."

I gave Miranda a dollar, and she gave me a ticket. When she left I turned to Leo. "What's policy?"

He squished his eyebrows, and looked at me strangely.

"No really, I have no idea what she's talking about." I answered his questioning expression.

"It's a little like betting on horses through a bookie, and it's illegal. The policy bank or headquarters in this area is run by Duke Wilson. That's where they get the winning numbers."

Miranda approached the table with coffee pot in hand. As she poured us her fresh brewed coffee with the hint of cinnamon, she smiled and said, "He's right. All you gotta do is pick the same three numbers the balls in the cage pick."

"Like bingo," I asked.

"Sorta," she said. "But you need help picking out the numbers. I can help you find your own lucky numbers."

"Miranda, how often do you win?"

She gave out a big whooping laugh and left our table.

Phil leaned over and whispered, "She gets a cut from the bookie for every ticket she sells."

"Where else do they sell the tickets?"

"Almost everywhere in this neighborhood, but on the quiet, because it's illegal."

"The drugstore?"

"No way. Abe won't let Duke near the store. They had a falling out."

As I savored my pancakes my eyes fixed on an unusual scene; in the corner of the restaurant, Abe stood conversing in automated but whispered tones with a tall, impeccably dressed light brown -skinned young man. I turned to Leo, pointing in their direction. "Who's he talking to?"

"Alderman Johnson," Leo answered in between spoonfuls of grits.

"What gives? I've never seen him so quiet and secretive."

"Business meeting. Democratic convention in Chicago next summer, and elections coming up. Abe's wife comes from a powerful Democratic family."

Leo then folded open his newspaper and lapsed into silence, alerting me that there would be no more conversation on the subject. I watched the alderman pick up a leather briefcase, open it, and pass something to Abe. He left, and Abe moved through the room, greeting everyone on the way to his table.

WHEN MY DAY ENDED DURING rush hour, I usually followed the smells of garlic and lemon coming from the restaurants in Greek Town. They were worth the extra walk. I became a regular at Diana's, a grocery store with a restaurant in the back. I loved their spinach pie, their Greek chicken, and the owner Pete's greeting of, "God bless America." It was nice to hear somebody who was still patriotic, even though it always sounded like a Greek message.

I was sitting at one of their small, Formica-topped tables enjoying my dinner and my glass of Roditis when I became aware of someone standing next to me.

"You alone?"

Looking up, my eyes locked on a stocky, gruff-looking, bald, sixty or so year-old man. A cigarette dangled from his fingers, and a monkey wrench was sticking out of his back pocket. A large round head with a ruddy nose usually found on alcoholics found its way to my face.

"You're new. I hear you're working for Abe too. Watch out for him." Before I could respond, he straightened up and headed for the exit.

I turned to my regular waiter and asked, "George, who was that?"

"That's Max Roy. He's the dentist across the street from the drugstore. He's been here forever. He's a little crazy, fast to anger though."

I vaguely remembered seeing him leave the drugstore in a huff one day.

The next day Leo filled me in on Roy. I learned that Dr. Roy, an ex-heavyweight fighter, was the only occupant left in the medical building across the street from my office. He was no longer married. If he had children he never talked about them. His office was open six days a week. He spent a huge amount of time in the drugstore arguing with Abe Meyer. I admired him for sticking it out in a community like Skid Row for over twenty-five years. I had been there six months, and I was beginning to believe I wouldn't make it through the year. All my idealism was running short.

# CHAPTER 7

To KEEP MY SANITY, PLEASE my fiancée, and to supplement my income, I was now working two days a week in a friend's suburban office. I put an ad in the paper for help in my Madison Street office. I was hoping to find someone who might want to buy the office. Gary Grisby answered the ad. I set him up to work on Tuesdays and Thursdays.

Before Dr. Grisby finished his first day of work, I received an SOS call from Abe. "You managed to hire someone crazier than the people living in the area."

I met Abe at the pharmacy and we went up to the dental office.

Upon entering the office, I had a hard time containing my laughter. Dr. Grisby, about thirty, short, thin, and bald, was dressed in green fatigues, combat boots, a surgical mask, and rubber surgical gloves.

"Gary, what gives with the outfit?" I asked.

"What do you mean outfit? I've accepted a job in a war zone, and I've dressed for it."

"Gary, this won't work. You're scaring the patients."

From the sidelines in his normal booming voice, Abe yelled, "Cut the crap. The guy is nuts. He's been giving lectures to the bums about something called recycling and about eating fruit!"

I turned back to Gary. "What lectures?"

"The only reason I accepted this job was to do a good deed," Gary answered with indignation.

"Get rid of him, Mel."

Pointing a finger at Abe in a trembling voice, Gary yelled back, "I'll get even with you."

I felt like I was in the crossfire of a war zone.

"Abe, please go downstairs and let me take care of it," I said.

I settled with Dr. Grisby, paying him for the full day, and escorted him to his car. Years later, when dentists were required to wear gloves and masks, I thought about him.

Abe came up to my office right before closing probably to check that Grisby was gone.

"What a nut case. Glad he's gone." He then waved two tickets in front of me. "Front and center seats to the White Sox's opener. Can you use them?"

I smiled. "You know how to tempt me. I love the White Soxs."

While putting his arm around my shoulders, he said, "Don't get your hopes up for a win. Oh, the next doctor you hire, let him know he has to write some scripts."

The next dentist I hired was a Dr. Panzer. The patients loved him, but I had to let him go as well. Dr. Panzer suggested that it would be a good idea to use nitrous oxide on the patients who were afraid of the dentist. Business increased initially. Then his business took a dive. I decided to stop by the office to see what was going on. Upon entering the office, I was pleased to see so many patients in the waiting room. I approached Darlene.

"It looks like business is booming. Where is Dr. Panzer, treating a patient?'

"Not really, Doctor."

"The door to the operatory is closed. Is he eating lunch?"

"He's busy."

Not liking the answers I was getting, thinking behind the closed door he might be entertaining a girl, I broke into the operatory.

Passed out on the dental chair from self-induced nitrous, Dr. Panzer was barely breathing.

"Darlene, call the paramedics!" I yelled as I tried to get the mask off of him and to revive him.

The office quickly cleared as the paramedics came rushing up the stairs. After reviving Dr. Panzer, they took him to County Hospital.

After they left I took a deep breath and sat down in an effort to pull myself together. I really thought he was dead.

I then turned to Darlene. "Was this an accident?"

"No," she said, "he used the nitrous every day. It was his high."

"Darlene, why didn't you tell me what was going on in the office?"

"Not my business what the doctor do."

Suddenly, I became aware of her bruised face, and I panicked. "Where did you get that black eye? It wasn't from Dr. Panzer, was it?"

"No way. Tyrone got high again and knocked me around."

"Why do you stay with him?" I asked. She stared at me, shook her head, and went back to the desk.

The thought that Tyrone was hitting Darlene didn't hold well with me. I was leery of him, not only because of his total lack of a moral conscience. I was still learning about addicts willing to do anything for a fix, but I somehow felt this was Tyrone's nature on or off of drugs. I tolerated him basically because he was a package deal with Darlene, and I was really afraid of making him and his gang-related friends my enemy.

Almost on clue, Tyrone walked through the front door holding a beautiful bouquet of red and yellow roses.

"For my girl."

Darlene just stood there with her eyes wide open. I think she was in shock. Realizing I didn't want to know where the expensive flowers came from, I moved to my lab, leaving the two of them alone. From my room I heard some sort of an apology coming from Tyrone.

" Didn't want to hurt ya, but you don't know when to shut your trap. With Spider you need to watch it."

"Oh, Tyrone, you done got hooked on that damn coke, and you don't know what you're doing anymore. You keep hanging out with the Rangers and Spider you gonna end up as a dead nigger or in jail.

Ignoring her, he smiled and asked, "Heh, you like the flowers?"

"They sweet."

Listening to this conversation made me realize that Tyrone and Darlene were just like any other couple, only they had the misfortune to be in an environment that promoted drugs, crime, and violence. Leo had told me that Tyrone's mother was a prostitute and his dad was long gone. Without a parent to push education and morals, it was almost impossible for him to escape his destiny. Darlene was trying. Why, even her speech changed when she talked to me versus her contemporaries. I thought about getting her into a dental assistants program.

Later that afternoon, when Clancy, the cop came in, I learned the real tale of the roses.

"Doc, I'm sorry I missed my appointment this morning, but a flower delivery truck broke down on Madison Street, and the kids were stealing everything they could get their hands on. That poor white delivery guy was hiding on the floor of the truck when we pulled up in the squad car. Two tires were gone, and the truck was sitting lopsided."

I smiled as I saw Darlene quickly hide her flowers under the desk.

"No problem, Clancy, get in the chair and we'll take care of you."

THE CALL CAME IN THE middle of the night. I jumped out of bed, rushed into the kitchen, and grabbed the phone in an effort to keep it from waking my folks. Expecting ADT, telling me the office alarm went off, I was stunned to hear someone say, "This is the County Hospital. James

Garrison has listed you as next of kin. He's in critical condition from a stab wound."

It took me a few minutes to connect James Garrison to Jim Bones. I threw on a pair of jeans and a T-shirt and quickly ran out to my car, only to return home. Seeing as it was the beginning of March and two in the morning, I realized I needed a jacket and I needed to leave my folks a note so they wouldn't worry. The drive was easy, not much traffic on a Sunday at that hour, until I reached the exit on Roosevelt Road, where the streets were screaming from the ambulances and police car sirens.

County Hospital, housed in a magnificent terra cotta building, which covered at least one square block, was built at the turn of the century as a teaching hospital and a place for the poor of the city to receive care. It was still operating at full capacity. The inside, with its thirty to forty end patient wards and its crowded, small rooms, was showing its age, with ancient porcelain on metal equipment and its layers and layers of white-painted walls and its narrow concrete and metal stairs.

Walking by the emergency room on my way to Jim's room I felt like I was in a war zone. Blood was everywhere due to stabbings, gunshot wounds, and accidents. Moans and cries were heard throughout the halls. I stood back against the wall as a gurney with a young girl was rushed into the ward. Her arm hung down over the stretcher, while an oxygen mask covered her face.

"Accident?" I asked the fireman when he emerged from the double doors.

"Another prostitute beat up," he answered as he continued walking out the door, as if it was an every night occurrence.

I continued down the hall in search of Jim, no longer surprised at anything.

I almost didn't recognize the quiet, blank stare from the sad looking man sitting outside of Jim's room.

"Abe, what are you doing here?"

Before I could talk to Abe, the nurse motioned to me. "Jim wants to talk to you."

I entered the hospital room. His body looked frail and drawn, while his face was white and bloated and his breathing shallow. Jim Bones had lost a fight over a bag of heroin. It turns out the winner was in another ward dying of tainted dope. Jim beckoned to me. I leaned down as he whispered,

"My family is in Glencoe. Let them know that I wasn't all bad, that I helped you. Go with Abe."

I bowed my head in an affirmative motion as I watched him take his last breath. I left the hospital room with tears running down my face.

The nurse looked at me through a resigned face. "This one was different. He's been here before. I thought he would pull through again."

"He overdosed before?"

"A lot of bad stuff out there. This is County Hospital, we see everything."

As she walked away toward a gurney carrying a stab-wound victim, I wondered how she worked here.

Abe and I walked out together. By my car, he said, "I'll call the Garrisons. We'll get his things and take them out to their house tomorrow."

I drove home and fell into bed only moments before my dad got up. Working on only three hours of sleep, I met Abe at the drugstore, and we drove out together to see Mr. and Mrs. James Garrison II. Abe was quiet as we drove along the outer drive past icy Lake Michigan with its three-foot waves breaking against the rocks.

"No jokes today, Abe?" I asked.

"I'm going to miss that kid. I hoped he would one day come to his senses."

"He was different from the others, very intelligent." I answered, "Do you know his family?"

"No, just that they are very rich WASPS."

We parked on Sheridan Road in Glencoe. Got out of the car, buttoned up our coats, put on our hats and gloves, and walked the path to what we thought was the Garrison home. Instead, we were greeted by the chauffeur who informed us, "Sorry, gentlemen, this is the servant's quarters. The main house is down there on the lake. You can drive it."

We continued to walk at least two more blocks before approaching a large, white-columned red brick Colonial mansion sitting on a cliff above Lake Michigan, surrounded by manicured gardens that must have been beautiful in the summer. Abe hit the lion-head brass knocker attached to a solid oak door. A cute, petite maid in a proper black-and-white uniform greeted us and led us down a hall, surrounded with what must have been original masterpieces, to a large, dark wood-paneled library with built-in shelves holding hundreds of books. The maid motioned for us to sit down on the yellow silk brocade sofa. We did very stiffly. Looking around, I thought about the flophouse where we redeemed Jim's belongings. It was a filthy, roach- infested place with flaking wallpaper, sealed windows, rows of beds, and one bathroom per twenty inhabitants. *Why was he there, instead of in this beautiful home*? I wondered.

Mrs. Garrison, dressed in a white silk blouse, black skirt, low-heeled shoes, and a pearl choker, entered the library. In a very formal, cool, detached voice, she thanked us for coming and showed us pictures of a handsome young man neither one of us recognized.

"James had so much promise. He was a Rhodes Scholar. He was patriotic and very innocent. He joined the army, went to Vietnam, and came back a drug addict. We tried so hard with therapy and rehabs before he disappeared. I haven't seen or heard from him in six years. His father considered him dead, but I still had hope. He was only thirty-one."

Giving her his small packet of belongings, I said, "Mrs. Garrison, he was still a very nice, caring, intelligent person who had an addiction he couldn't lick. I would like to be at the funeral. Please let me know what the arrangements will be." I handed her my card with my phone number.

"That's nice of you, Doctor, but there will be no public display. We will bury him privately with the immediate family. My husband is the CEO of a prominent company, and we need to keep this to ourselves. I hope you and Mr. Meyer will honor our feelings."

Listening to her gave me the feeling that for this family, James had died years ago, and they weren't interested in acknowledging his existence, dead or alive. Abe got up from the chair and looked down at Mrs. Garrison. In a calm, steady voice, he said, "It sounds like you are more concerned with appearances than your son."

In a cold, steady voice, she answered, "I believe it's time for you to leave."

We were led out of the room by the same cute maid. Walking by a silver coffee service with miniature pastries, I leaned into Abe. "You could have saved your comments until we were served those goodies." He burst out laughing. "I'll take you for some real food."

Walking back to the car, Abe shook his head and hit his right fist against his left arm. "High falutin' schmuck. They have another son, toes the line, works for the bank, married in the right circle, and lives in Lake Forest."

I turned toward Abe. "You've met them before?"

"No, just talked to the cold fish. Tried to get them to pick up Jim, or let me bring him out to them. She hung up on me. I tried to get him to the rehab clinic, offered him a decent room, but he was hooked."

"Abe, with a mother like that, I get the feeling Jim was messed up even before going to Vietnam."

Before getting in on the driver's side, Abe took his keys out of his pocket and opened the passenger door for me. We drove south on Sheridan Road. Abe pulled off on Morris Avenue and stopped the car by a delicatessen called Ashkenazi.

"Now you'll get some real food."

The place was packed with people, even in the middle of the afternoon. Abe greeted several of them on our way to a table in the center of the room. He ordered for the both of us; chopped liver, chicken soup, corned beef sandwiches, and chocolate phosphates to consume there, and rugalech to take out. While stuffing myself with food, I asked Abe, "Why do you stay in the Skid Row area? It can't be for the money."

"I was born on Maxwell Street. One of eight kids, worked every day of my life since I was ten. Didn't need schooling in those days. You got your education on the streets." He stopped and smiled after that comment, something like my dad did when he was reminiscing. He turned to me. "Mel, were your parents from the West Side?"

"My mom and dad were South Siders, but my dad's family came from the West Side, and he loves going to Maxwell Street to shop."

"Mel, someday I'll show you the real Maxwell Street." He then continued telling his story. "As a teenager, I worked as a soda jerk for old man Bloom in the same store I own now."

"As what?" I asked.

He gave me one of his hardy laughs and a pat on the shoulder. "You're so young. I made the sundaes and sodas in the store when the liquor counter was a beautiful soda fountain, and the West Side was in its glory. My creations were better than that place on Eighty-seventh Street called Melody Lane. I bought the store after pharmacy school even though the neighborhood was changing."

His eyes were glazed over and there was a smile on his face as he recalled what must have been a better time in his life.

A chubby, gray-bearded old timer grabbed Abe and gave him a hug. "What are you doing here on a weekday?"

Abe smiled and returned the hug. "Moshe, meet my friend Mel."

We exchanged hellos, and Moshe moved on to the next table. Abe turned to me, "We were at Midway together. You know, Mel, nobody I know from the war ended up as crazy as these guys coming back from Vietnam."

"My dad said the same thing. He doesn't understand the war protests, or the drug scenes. He said when he and my uncles came back from Europe they were proud of their accomplishments, and they were greeted by a grateful, jubilant country. Look at what happened to James. I guess you saw the same potential in him that I did. What a shame," I said.

"He reminded me of my son."

Abe, I didn't know you had a son. I've only heard you talk about your daughter and your three granddaughters."

"My eighteen-year-old son overdosed on drugs ten years ago."

I looked at him totally in shock.

"But Abe ... you're constantly helping the guys on the street feed their habit."

"By the time the addicts end up on Skid Row, they're goners. I like to think I'm giving them a little happiness. I know I can't reform them at that stage."

"But you tried to help James," I added softly.

That day I saw a different Abe than the one I knew on Madison Street.

# CHAPTER 9

TRAVELING THIRTY MILES EACH MORNING to the office from my home on the South East side of Chicago seemed normal. It was the early sixties, so it never occurred to me to leave my family and move into my own apartment. My mother was already lamenting about her only child's coming marriage and move to the north side of Chicago. Madison Street in downtown Chicago represented the Mason/Dixon Line separating the North Siders of the city from the South Siders. The best explanation of this is the war between the South Side White Sox's fans, and the North Side Cub's fans. Cindy, my fiancée, had only been to my parents' home once. The closest she ever came to the south side was a trip to downtown Chicago.

CINDY AND I HAD BEEN downtown to see *The Sound of Music* at the Michael Todd Theatre and to Johnnie's Steak House for dinner. After dropping her off in Northbrook, I returned home around two in the morning. My mother greeted me at the door.

"Your office was broken into."

"Are you sure? Abe gets a lot of false ADT calls."

"The pharmacist called. Dad is getting dressed. He will drive down there with you."

Abe and the police were in the building when we arrived. The robbers had bypassed the alarm by cutting a hole in the roof of the back poker room. My office was fine, except for a broken door pane. I was only missing ten dollars from petty cash and some codeine from the dental cabinet. The thief knew where to look.

"What about Phil's office?" I asked.

"It's fine. They know he never keeps any money or drugs around. He gets all his drugs from me," Abe answered. "Actually, I'm surprised they bothered with your place."

The first thought that came to my mind was Tyrone, or Spider, but I didn't want to accuse them with no proof.

Looking around, Abe shook his head. "Most of the time the alarm goes off and I come down here for nothing. This time they figured out how to get around it."

The drugstore part was fine, but the pharmacy was another story. It was a mess, with drawers opened and contents thrown everywhere. The thieves were looking for something specific.

Abe came out of the back room looking alarmed.

"Besides drugs and five hundred bucks, my gun is missing. It was hidden in a drawer."

"Maybe Dave took it," I volunteered.

"No, I called him."

Abe and a police officer named Mike were uneasy about the missing gun. It was the sixties, and the West Side of the city was becoming increasingly dangerous now that the country was in the middle of the civil rights movement and the anti-war rallies.

Abe turned to the policeman. "This was a robbery for the gun. If you don't find the gun someone will be shot!"

The policeman answered him, "I think you're right. Junkies will take anything and everything when they need a fix. Whoever broke in here left the stuff easy to sell like the radios and the typewriter."

It was nearly four in the morning by the time we made it home. My dad only said one sentence on the way.

"Mel, I didn't send you to school to end up where I started, or worse, in the morgue.

Cindy was already on my case. Now my dad was too, but I wasn't ready to give up. I had grown to think of my patients as my friends, and I wasn't afraid of the neighborhood. Maybe I was just being very naïve.

THE SOUND OF SIRENS AND fire trucks in the neighborhood was a daily occurrence, so I paid little attention to the fire truck outside my window one Tuesday morning, until I saw bright orange flames engulfing the building across the street.

I left my office and hurried down the steps to join the crowd standing behind the barriers set up by the fire department. We stood there, coughing from the smoke, silently watching the firemen work to save the building. Smoke was primarily coming out of the second-floor dental office belonging to Dr. Roy. No one was in the building except for a few bums who had been using the empty first floor for shelter. They were exiting the building coughing and dragging their meager belongings. Dr. Roy, the only legal occupant, had been off that day and couldn't be reached until the fire was raging full force. After detecting some rumbling, the fireman cleared the area. When the fire was out I couldn't believe the extent of the damage. The floor had caved in, and the second-floor office was now in the basement. A three-hundred-pound dental chair was lying on its side, and an old wooden cabinet was completely wrecked. All Dr. Roy's equipment and records had been destroyed. The word on the street was that the fire had been deliberately set. Fortunately no one was hurt.

Feeling sorry for Dr. Roy, I walked over to him, and offered my help and my office.

"Dr. Roy, I'm Dr. Greenberg, and I have a dental office above the drugstore. We met briefly before. I don't use my office on Tuesdays and Thursdays. You're welcome to use it until your office is put back together. I'm sure that Darlene, my assistant, would be happy to help you."

He stuck out his arm to shake my hand.

"Offer accepted. I knew you were a decent sort."

When I told Tyrone and Darlene Dr. Roy would be using the office two days a week, they were not happy.

"Abe is not going to like Roy in his building," said Tyrone.

"He's right, they've been feuding over script money," said Phil as he entered the office, leaving a trail of ashes from his cigar. Phil, the 350-pound physician who shared the second floor with me, ate all my donuts, gave me advice, and routinely sent patients down stairs with six prescriptions, sat down on the contour dental chair, leaned back, and said, "You're not busy. These chairs are great for napping."

"Phil, you can hardly breathe. As doctor to doctor, cut down on the food and the smoking."

Opening one eye, he grinned at me. "Mel, did you know that in my past life I was a diet doctor?'

"Tell me the true story."

"No, really. Back in the early fifties I had a diet clinic on Peterson, a wife, and a kid too."

"What happened?"

"Alcohol, divorce, and then food. About ten years ago when no one would hire me, Abe set me up above the drugstore."

Darlene came into the operatory. "Real patient with a toothache in the waiting room."

As I watched Phil struggle out of the chair, I looked past the fat and saw dark, curly hair, sparkling brown eyes, white-capped teeth, and neat, clean clothes on a friendly, nice fifty-year-old.

"The word is the godfathers of Madison Street burned down Roy's building," said Tyrone.

"What are you talking about?"

"You are really dumb, white boy."

"Tyrone, don't talk to the doctor like that. Ain't you got no respect?" Darlene stated.

Tyrone whirled around and threw Darlene across the room. Standing over her in a tense tone of voice, he yelled, "Shut your trap, girl."

Angry and probably not thinking, I grabbed him. "Get out of my office."

He backed away toward the door. "Okay, Doc, don't get rattled. She my woman."

Enraged, I repeated myself. "Out!"

"Okay, Doc, we cool, right, Darlene?"

Darlene got up. "It's okay, Doctor. I'm fine."

Tyrone left, but not for good.

Junk became a desperate way of life. Tyrone was a junkie, and he scared me. Besides this scene with Darlene, my petty cash drawer was always missing money, and I suspected he was using my office to make his purchases and sales.

About a week later, returning to my office to retrieve a phone number, I walked in on Tyrone and his friend Spider. Afraid and angry, I confronted Tyrone.

"Tyrone, what are you doing in my office?"

He gave me a cocky answer. "Hey, man, stay cool. Spider and I just taking care of some business. We leaving." Spider eyed me with little curiosity or concern.

I called the locksmith the next day and made arrangements for him to come and change the locks on my door, even though I knew this would not keep Tyrone out. I didn't want to, but I contemplated firing Darlene, as she was so totally under his spell and headed for trouble.

I liked Spider less than Tyrone, because he was smarter and more daring than Tyrone. Earlier that week I observed Spider in the pawn shop nervously pacing while Leo looked over merchandise he had brought in.

"You know I don't take guns. Where did you get this watch? It has an inscription on it," said Leo, the pawnshop owner, folding his arms across his chest.

"It was my girlfriend's," Spider replied as he began to pace.

"What was her name?" Leo's eyes followed the young man from right to left.

Spider quickly grabbed for the watch, trying to look at the name. Leo snatched the watch, tossed it into the paper bag, and said, "Get out of here."

"You god damn fucker. What kind of pawn shop dealer are you?" Spider cursed as he left with his stuff.

"That one's no good. They should have never let him out," Leo said, shaking his index finger in the air.

"Out of where?" I asked.

"Spider spent eighteen months in Joliet for armed robbery. He got that scar while there."

"What scar?"

"Jesus, Mel. The one on his neck, going from ear to ear. You can't miss it. Did you come in to chat or do you need something?"

"I could use a copy machine if you ever get a good working one," I answered, rather annoyed at the way my friend was treating me.

"Most of the ones I usually get are leaking ink. I'll let you know if anything good comes in."

"Thanks. Do you want to get a bite after work?"

"It's Friday, poker game night. When are you going to join the weekly game?" Leo asked.

Every Friday night Abe conducted business in the back of the store. Then Leo, Phil, Clancy, Roy and his other neighborhood cronies ate corned beef sandwiches and played poker most of the night.

"I don't play cards," I answered. I didn't want to get involved in Abe's business.

"You're kidding," said Leo. "How did you ever get through school without playing?"

"I studied."

Of course, Abe and Leo didn't believe me. After weeks of refusing their offer I finally accompanied Leo to the back room of the pharmacy. As we entered, Clancy, chomping on a sandwich, stood guard at the door. Handing me a bottle of Miller's beer, Abe gave me a hug. "Heh, Mel, about time you joined us." Pointing to a table with a spread of deli sandwiches, beer, alcohol, and cakes, he said, "Delivered from Manny's Deli, only the best. Es (eat)."

I grabbed a sandwich and followed Leo to the big round card table, which was filled with ash trays, red, white, and blue chips, cash, cards, and glasses. The regulars were seated, ready to start. Abe put his arm around me. "I think you all know Mel. We're going to teach him poker." This got a laugh out of the group, which consisted of Phil, who gave me a smile, in-between bites, Leo nursing his beer, and Roy fidgeting with his chips in one hand, while a cigarette dangled from the other. Before I could be introduced to the fourth person sitting at the table, a distinguished-looking, tall, light-skinned black man impeccably dressed in a striped suit and a paisley tie entered.

Abe was all smiles as he grabbed the man's hand and led him to the food table. Looking at me, Abe said, "Mel, meet Alderman Johnson. This man will someday be a United States congressman."

Roy looked up, and said, "Full of shit. No offense, Mr. Johnson, but no black man will ever be a United States congressman!"

# CHAPTER 10

THE NEXT WEEK, ABE SHOWED up in my office. "Mel, I promised to show you the real Maxwell Street. Meet me here Sunday."

Abe was all smiles when I walked into the store Sunday morning at 9:30 am. Due to Chicago's liquor laws, the store couldn't sell alcohol on Sundays until noon, so they didn't open until then. We would have two hours to explore Chicago's famous market.

We drove the mile and a half south on Halsted Street to Maxwell Street. Even though the height of the market's activity was from the turn of the century to the 1950s, there were still crowds of people this Sunday in 1968.

Abe walked along greeting people in the stores, and at the stalls, while pointing out special locations to me. "Mel, on this corner was Dunn's Hat Shop, and here was Wexler's Shoes, and here Grace's Leather Goods store is still in business. Do you want a jacket? Their leather is still the best, and I can get you a special price.

"I was born around the corner on Johnson Street, later called Peoria. With ten of us crowded into a few rooms, you had to get along. We bickered and shouted at each other, made a lot of noise, but nothing serious. If you wanted a real fight, the Italians were just a ways north, and the Irish, just a ways south."

We stopped on the northwest corner of Maxwell and Halsted. Abe grabbed my arm and pointed to the corner. "Right here my father, Herschel Meyerstein, from Romania, opened the first hotdog stand. He sold Vienna hot dogs with the mustard, pickle, and tomatoes. Business was so good that the politicians forced him to turn over his stand to them. I was only ten years old, but on that day, I learned the power of politics and money, especially in Chicago, and I made a vow to never let something like that happen to me."

"How did you make sure it never happened to you?"

Abe laughed. "I married the politician's daughter."

We walked across the street to a hot dog push cart. "Harry, fix us up with two big dogs." Slapping me on the back, he turned to Harry and said, "This is my friend, Doctor Greenberg. He thinks Carl's on the south side has the best dogs. Show him he's wrong." Soon my hands were full of two large hotdogs dripping in mustard, green pickle relish, large tomato slices, and onions slices, on a poppy seed bun. Abe looked at me and smiled. Turning to Harry, he said, "You forgot the orange pop."

As I chomped on my hot dog, Abe said, "Good, right? Natural casing and chartreuse piccalilli!"

"Abe," a portly, full-faced, grey-bearded Caucasian said and threw his arms around my friend. They engaged in a heated Yiddish conversation, using their hands almost as much as their lips. When Abe's friend left, Abe turned to me. "He used to be one of the best pushers, while his brother was the puller. They stood outside of their father's clothing goods store and brought in the business. Spent fifteen dollars there for a suit for my graduation from pharmacy school. Most money I ever spent on clothes back then. His brother became a judge, and he an ambulance chaser."

Abe continued to talk, while pointing to a line of stores. "The back rooms of these stores were where the action took place. If you knew the right people you were let in to join the games: poker, craps, horses, jukeboxes, booze. I was a runner for a few years."

I enjoyed the history lesson Abe was giving me. I always thought Maxwell Street was just a market for the poor, and the bargain hunter. As we passed several stalls occupied by blacks and Spanish, Abe greeted them before whispering to me, "This street was all Jewish in my day." When he stopped and looked across the intersection of Halsted and Maxwell, I could tell he was in another place, even though he was still talking to me. "Mel, I can still see the wagons, pushcarts, tables, and shoppers, waving their hands and shouting in their native Yiddish dialogues: the ragman to the fish vendor, the hagglers, and the bargain hunters, and most of all, the crowds.

"The immigrants who ended on Maxwell Street dreamed that their children would succeed, and most of them did. The candy store owner's son became a federal judge. One cigar-maker's son became head of CBS, and his partner's son became the brains behind Al Capone. A trucking store magnate's father owned a chicken store right here on Maxwell Street, and an ambassador to the UN's father peddled.

"Countless of my friends became lawyers. We all stay in touch. Nothing can compare to growing up on Maxwell Street and the adjoining Vest Side!"

The moment was broken when Abe looked at his watch. "Time to go. They'll be lined up at the store's door, ready for their drinks. Yesterday was welfare check day."

# CHAPTER 11

BY THE END OF MARCH Dr. Roy's office was put together enough for him to return to it, and I was very happy to see him go. He never offered me any money for the use of my office, my supplies, and my girl, and his gruff mannerisms and take-control attitude left me tense around him. I usually stayed away from the place on the days he was there. When Phil told me Roy was selling needles from my office, I became enraged.

Abe stopped by. "Son, you put me in a bad position by letting Roy use your office. It's my building, and I'd like to know who is using the offices."

"You're right, Abe," I answered as I cleaned up the office, and threw out the garbage, papers, and cigar ashes Dr. Roy had left.

"You know, you got the first year free. We need to talk about rent for next year, since you aren't writing enough scripts," Abe added to the conversation.

"Fine," I answered, while thinking there probably wouldn't be a next year.

"By the way, I asked, is Phil all right? I haven't seen him around."

"He's fine. I have a young kid that might take over his space. We need some new blood around here."

I wasn't really happy with this conversation. Abe had been acting strange lately, leaving the store for stretches at a time, finding fault with everyone, just not being his fun, friendly normal self. After work I stopped in the store and bought some candy and a coke. While paying, I asked Sandra, "Something going on I don't know about? Abe isn't acting right. He's nervous, and always too busy to stop and tell a joke."

"I agree, but I don't know nothing." I shook my head and left. Sandra never knows anything. That must be why Abe keeps her around.

AT A LATER DATE I would learn that other people in the neighborhood were under stress, also.

Two teenagers sat on a cot in a small, cold basement apartment, a black gang jacket laid at the foot of the bed. The shorter, thinner boy handed the tall, muscular one a black wool cap and a small hand gun. The muscular one picked up the Smith and Wesson. His hands were shaking, while his wide open eyes just stared at the gun. He turned to his companion. "I can't do it. You better go."

The shorter one got up. "You the man that owes the money. I do it, I keep the money. Don't worry. Nothing to it. Nobody on the street gonna interfere. Nigger, don't blow this. The man wouldn't like that!"

The tall, muscular male put the gun down, rolled up his sleeves, and started to shake all over. "I need something. What you got?"

IN THE DRUGSTORE, THE PHARMACIST, Dave Miller, was busy in the back of the store filling out paperwork. He stopped and looked at his watch. *Where is Abe?* he thought. *He promised to be back in time for me to leave early. My wife will kill me if I miss her niece's bas mitzvah.*

One of the clerks knocked on the door. Dave opened it. "Dave, some guy came in and asked for you. Should I bring him back here?"

"No, I'll come up front." Dave put down his pen and walked out of the office.

On the way to the front of the store, Dave said to himself. *"I should tell him to come back. I don't deal with the customers or the salesmen, Abe does."*

The tall, muscular teen with his head down looked familiar. "What do you …"

Dave never got to finish the sentence. The kid pulled a gun out of his jacket. At the sight of a gun, the two clerks and the one customer ducked. When they recovered, the gunman was gone and Dave Miller was lying on the floor in a pool of blood. His black wig hanging half on and half off of his head was now streaked with red, and his normal impeccably clean pharmacy coat was bloodied. Sandra screamed, while a man ran out of the store yelling for help.

Sy was shuffling down the street, eyes on the sidewalk, hoping to find a few cents or a cigarette butt when he was knocked down by a large male running out of the drugstore. Before Sy could recover, the guy jumped on the stopped bus and disappeared. Grumbling, Sy started to pick himself up, but he was knocked down again by several people rushing out of the drugstore.

"What the hell is wrong with you people?" Sy yelled.

"Sy, Dave's been shot. Did you see anyone?" Sandra asked.

Soon, an ambulance pulled up and the street became crowded with curious onlookers. Sy quietly moved on, mumbling to himself, *Too bad. Don't want to get questioned. No way, no way. Didn't see nothing.*

Abe was smiling about his successful meeting with the alderman. He turned off the expressway and pulled up to his store. Alarmed at the commotion outside of the store, he stopped the car in the middle of the street, got out, broke through the police barricade, and ran toward the ambulance. Shocked when he realized Dave was dead, he sat down on the curb and put his head in his hands. Later in the store, talking to the police, he accepted their analysis that it must have been a drug robbery gone wrong. After all, Dave had no enemies. He did, not Dave. Before closing the store, he took a drink of Jack Daniels. It wasn't going to be easy telling Dave's wife Edith. *We've been friends for over forty years,* Abe thought.

THE DRUGSTORE WAS CLOSED ON Monday. With my window open on the clear warm spring day, I could hear customers below pulling at the door and complaining, even thought there was a sign that said, "Closed for my friend Dave Miller's funeral." I guessed that most of the Skid Row customers forgot how to read, or they didn't care. I wasn't much better. I couldn't bring myself to go to the funeral. I sent flowers and rationalized that I hardly knew Dave.

Tuesday, the drugstore opened, but it wasn't business as usual. Abe didn't make his rounds, and his booming, friendly voice was nowhere to be heard. From then on he stationed himself in the back of the store filling prescriptions and doing paperwork.

A few days later I entered the store and asked Sandra, "Do they have any suspects? Did you recognize the shooter?"

"Mel, once I saw that gun, I ducked to save my ass."

"Sandra, did the guy really escape on the bus?"

"Yeah, no get-away car. That's why they think it was some young punk needing drugs."

"How's Abe doing?"

"Not good. He never comes out of the pharmacy."

I walked to the back and knocked on the pharmacy door. Abe opened it. "Abe, I just wanted to say I'm really sorry about Dave."

He looked up at me with watery eyes. "Me too." Trying to get back his usual manner, he said, "This damn paperwork is grating my nerves. I haven't done it in thirty years."

"Why don't you hire someone to help?"

He smiled and ruffled the hair on my head. "My sweet, innocent boy. Go, write some scripts to make me feel better."

AN INVESTIGATION WAS STARTED, BUT this was in a neighborhood where crime was rampant and informers were nonexistent, so the investigation was soon put on the back burner. Because a middle-class white man was shot, the *Chicago Tribune* gave it a column on the third page. If it had been a black man shot on Skid Row, the story wouldn't have made the news at all.

I was amazed that no one on the street talked about Dave's murder. The police were busy thinking about the increasing number of young Vietnam War protestors.

Then, about three weeks later, on a bright, sunny April Fool's Day, 1967, while working on a patient, we were interrupted by sirens from a fire truck blasting through the air. At first we thought business as usual, but when the blast became louder and the truck jolted to a stop in front of our building, we took notice and bolted out of the building, even though no smoke or flames were visible. Downstairs we joined a crowd of people standing behind a police barricade. We watched policemen, coroners, detectives, photographers, and ambulances coming and going outside the drugstore. When a gurney came out carrying a lifeless body face down, my heart sank. The short, plumb, bald body clothed in a bloodstained pharmacy coat was easy to identify, even though it was partially covered by a sheet. An uncanny quiet fell on the crowd as they moved apart to form a passageway for the two firemen.

Abe's dead body was being lifted into the ambulance when the silence was shattered by a scream. All eyes turned toward the tall, black figure breaking through the police barricade and landing on top of the gurney. When the police untangled him, he was chanting, "No, no, don't go, Doc. I'll pay you what I owe, just don't leave me." Lucious uttered the sentiment of the stunned crowd standing around the store.

From the accounts of witnesses, the same man that killed Dave entered the store and asked for Abe. When Abe came out, he shot him and again fled by foot and disappeared.

THE POLICE WERE NOW FORCED to do a thorough investigation. Policemen, plainclothesmen, and newsmen were everywhere. The drugstore was closed, and the natives of Madison Street were nervous and restless. They were truly homeless without the pharmacists and the store. Most used the store as their post office and were now without their welfare and disability checks.

"I'm getting out of here," Sy moaned. "The police are crazy. They hauled me down to the station for spitting on the street. Then they went and threatened me. If I didn't tell them who done the killing they would jail me. They couldn't hold me more than overnight. I got my rights."

No one was safe. The street was the quietest it had ever been. Everybody was hiding. If they knew who did the killings, they weren't talking. Informers didn't live long here. Most mourned the loss of the pharmacy. Abe and Dave had been like family taking care of their needs. Throughout the next few days, bewildered people would try to open the locked store. There was no place for the homeless to get their food, wine, and tobacco fix, especially on credit.

I missed my conversation breaks with Abe and the tumult coming from the drugstore. I never really knew Dave, but in the last nine months Abe had become my friend.

I recalled how when I first opened my office things would happen on the street that would shock me to the point of disbelief. Eight months later I found myself standing watching buildings burn, bums bleeding from stab wounds, or men fighting for food or cigarette butts like it was routine, but Abe's shooting had saddened and scared me. I wanted to go back to my safe world in my parents' house on the southeast side of Chicago.

LEO AND I WENT TO Abe's funeral at Weinstein's Funeral Home on Chicago's North Side. The funeral parlor was so full that several people had to stand during the service. As I viewed the crowd, I saw blacks and whites, shabby clothes, and expensive furs. I recognized Phil, Dr. Roy, Miranda, Lucious, Sandra, Duke, Tiger, a few Black Rangers, Alderman Johnson, plus several other politicians. Abe touched people from all walks of life. After the service twenty-five cars followed the hearse down Chicago's side streets, winding west and south, until an hour later they pulled into Waldheim Cemetery and stopped by the family gravesite. The crowd left their cars, gathered around the empty grave, and watched the workmen successfully lower the vault into it. The pallbearers walked over with the casket, and the workmen started to lower it into the grave. Halfway down the gears on the lowering mechanism stopped. After a few minutes of trying to get them to work, the workmen walked back to their truck to get some tools.

We stood around, cold and anxious to get the burial service over, when suddenly someone near the gravesite screamed, "Abe's coming out!"

All eyes turned to the gravesite. Like a scene in a horror movie, Abe's casket was moving up through the dirt hole to the top of the grave seemingly of its own volition. "No," yelled Abe's wife as she collapsed into her son-in-law's arms. Leo and I just stood there in awe, as others started to scatter.

The funeral director yelled, "Don't panic. It's only the machine moving the casket. Come back. The stuck gears have started to work on their own." Some people left, but most reluctantly returned, and order was restored to the group. Abe's wife was revived, and the burial proceeded. To break the tension, one of Abe's West Side friends yelled out, "Abe is still in control. Maybe he's not ready to go."

Another friend smiled and said, "I can just hear him telling this story for months."

The Rabbi, shaken, finished the service in record time, and we all left immediately.

It was a day of circling the city. The Shiva was in Abe's house in a northern suburb an hour away from the west side cemetery. While driving, I turned to Leo and said, "You know, I never believed in an afterlife before today, but now I'm not too sure about it."

Leo answered, "Why, do you really think Abe moved the casket?"

"Maybe. It would be the kind of joke he would do. Who screamed?"

"There were so many people. I wasn't close enough to tell. It sounded like a male voice, or a husky female's."

"In the movies, the scream would have come from the murderer!" I teased.

WE PULLED IN FRONT OF his house in the fashionable Northbrook Suburb, left the car, washed our hands with the customary water jug by the door, and entered the house with the rest of the mourners. Inside the house we made it to the lunch table, filled our plates with an assortment of deli foods, and found seats by a table in the family room. We interacted with a well-dressed middle-class family who seemed to have no idea what Abe's life was like in the store. His wife, Adele, had not been in the store in twenty years, and his daughter had never been there, so when Leo and I talked about life on Skid Row, they had no idea what we were talking about.

"We begged him to get out of the neighborhood for years before Dave died," Adele said. "He was a quiet but stubborn man. We didn't need the money." From the looks of the tasteful furnishings, expensive antiques, and extremely neat surroundings, we knew this was true.

The house was overflowing with people, most of whom we didn't know, so we didn't stay long. When I went upstairs to the bedroom to get my coat, my eyes fixed their gaze on the picture above the bed. It was a wedding picture, probably from the thirties. The man and woman in the picture were dressed in a black tux and white wedding gown. The groom was thin but muscular, with a full head of black hair. Except for the upturned, devilish smile I would have never recognized the groom as Abe.

Walking out of their house, I turned to Leo. "Did you get the feeling there were two Abes? Did she say quiet? Can you imagine Abe without a temper or a loud, booming voice?"

Leo gave a half smile, the most of a facial expression I'd seen on him. "For sure I never knew the one who lived in that house."

"Not bad," I said as I gazed back at the five-thousand-square-foot yellow brick house sitting on a one-acre lot.

Answering my own question, I said, "Maybe it was the only place he was free to be himself, Abe Meyerstein from Maxwell Street."

When I returned to my office, I was relieved to find the Skid Row area very quiet. It was like the bums and drug dealers had all disappeared, or were in hiding. Madison and Halsted Streets were empty, except for the police, who were everywhere. Chicago was Mayor Daley's town and he was incensed about the murders and increasing violence in the city. Even the war protestors and the occasional lost hippies were not to be seen. Daley had convinced the Democratic Party that Chicago was the ideal place for their presidential convention in the summer of 1968, and he wasn't going to let them change their minds.

DARLENE AND I SAT IN an empty office for most of the first week we were back at work. I sat every morning with my coffee, and Mike Royko's column from the *Chicago Daily News*, while Darlene nervously smoked one cigarette after another.

"Where's Tyrone?" I asked. "I haven't seen him around for days."

"Don't know," she answered.

I walked over to the window and looked onto the street below. The street was empty except for one old bum in dirty clothes and toes sticking out of tattered gym shoes. His mouth was moving, like he was having a conversation with someone, but no one else was on the street. All of a sudden I felt lonely and fearful. This was a different neighborhood without the drugstore.

My thoughts were interrupted by someone who called out, "Doc."

The man introduced himself as Detective Scarianno. He was a curious, chain-smoking, middle-aged white male. He said he needed to ask me a few question about the murders. When he finally left, I felt drained, and worried. He seemed to indicate that he regarded me, plus several other people on the street, suspects in the murders. I looked for Darlene.

"Darlene," I called.

No one answered. I looked around the office. Her purse and a lit cigarette were still on the desk. Strange, she never left without telling me. Maybe the detective scared her off. I was tempted by her cigarettes, but instead I gathered my belongings, locked up, and headed out the door. Reaching the bottom of the stairs, I jumped as a mouse scurried out of the locked drugstore.

Outside, I saw Leo. "Closing up early too? Want to go to Greek Town and sort out what's going on in this neighborhood?" I asked.

"How about the Vernon Park Tap? It's much quieter."

To add to my already doom and gloom mood, the skies opened up, and I found myself running to the car through a typical Chicago spring storm.

The Vernon Park Tap was a good choice. It was a dark tavern with a quiet restaurant in the back. I ordered a bottle of beer and a plate of spaghetti. Leo decided on a corned beef sandwich and a beer.

"Leo, you've been around a lot longer than I have. Who would want both druggists killed? I don't believe the holdup story, maybe once, but not twice. Somebody wanted to close the store and shut them up. Were they with the Mafia?"

Leo answered, "Not to my knowledge. Anyway, the Mafia doesn't work like that. They would have hired a professional."

"What about Duke Wilson, the numbers boss? He always scared me."

"Possible," Leo answered. "Last year he got mad as a dog at a poker game and never came back."

"Speaking of poker games, that alderman Johnson is becoming a big shot in the civil rights movement."

Leo ignored my comment about Johnson, and asked, "What about that crazy doctor who worked for you? Didn't he threaten Abe?"

"He was just crazy. What about Phil? Abe kicked him out and was going to put in a young physician. Forget it. Phil was too nice. Maybe Abe and Dave double-crossed the gang members."

Leo took a drink of beer and a bite of his sandwich before answering. When I first met him I had trouble getting used to his way of hesitating and thinking before speaking. "No, Abe was too smart for that. Dave kept a low profile. Abe had a game going with the scripts, but he was basically a good guy trying to help the bums."

"Good guy, you're crazy," said Max Roy. We hadn't seen him come in. "Abe was screwing everyone, black or white. That young punk killed him for a reason."

Leo and I looked up, shocked at Max Roy's presence and statement.

"Max, do you know something we don't?" Leo asked.

He gave us his usual disgusted, gruff look and left, as abruptly as he came, leaving behind a trail of ashes. Some had landed near my half-eaten bowl of spaghetti.

Knocking the ashes to the floor, I said, "Boy was I glad when he left my office. After he was there, it always smelled of smoke from his cigars and garlic from his sausages. He's really a strange one."

"Max has been around forever. He'll probably miss Abe and the drugstore more than anyone."

"How did you end up on Madison Street, Leo?"

"The pawn shop was my dad's. I just took over when he died. Been there fifteen years."

"Were you ever married?"

"No, I'm happy with my three cats and my train collection."

"You're still young. No romances or lost loves?"

"Actually, the only girl I ever cared about was Abe's daughter, but I wasn't good enough for the family."

"Really?" I answered, shocked.

Red streaks took over his face, and I could tell he was embarrassed. "Forget I said anything about it."

I quickly changed the subject. "Leo, have you ever been to Marshal Fields?"

"No, just Sears, and Goldblatt's, why?"

"It's an experience. Yesterday I met Cindy there to do something they call registering."

"Where they sign you up for wedding gifts?" he acknowledged, knowing what I was talking about.

"Leo, the place is different than any store I've ever been in. The building is beautiful with its stained glass tower window, and its signature clock. There's an ice cream shop in the store. Individual salesladies dressed in their Sunday best take care of you; everything is super clean and super expensive. My mom likes figurines and pretty dishes. She buys them at Goldblatt's, or at the corner store in South Chicago, for two, three dollars. My fiancée had me looking at dishes for twenty, thirty dollars apiece. I told her we could buy a set for twelve for that price. After about an hour I agreed to let her pick out everything and I would just show up."

"Where did you meet her?" Leo asked.

"Her dad's best friend was active with the University of Illinois dental school's alumni and got her a summer job there. I was in my third year working on cases, and we started to talk. Up until then I had a few girlfriends in high school, and at junior college. Nothing serious. In dental school I only had time to study. Cindy understood and hung around until graduation. Then we got engaged.

"She is a looker," Leo said as he put down his beer mug and glanced at his watch.

"Another beer?" the waiter asked.

"I better have some coffee. I'm driving the Dan Ryan," I said.

The Dan Ryan expressway running from Ninety-fifth Street to downtown Chicago, only open for a few years, was already known for its fast and reckless South Side drivers.

Leo regained his composure and smiled. "Another beer and you will have an easier time driving that expressway. When are you moving north?"

"Actually, Cindy has found an apartment in Glenview. My wedding is only two months from now. Keep June 20 open."

"Nice of you to plan to invite me, but I will probably feel out of place at a fancy wedding at the Drake."

"So will I, Leo," I admitted.

# Chapter 12

My dad was waiting for me at the door. In his hands was the *Chicago Tribune*. "City-wide Hunt for Druggists' Murderer." Pointing to it, he said, "I want you out of that neighborhood."

"So does Cindy," I said as I took the paper and entered the house. Looking at the headline, it struck me funny that Dave's murder brought little interest, while Abe's was all over the papers. I looked up as I realized my dad was still on the subject of me closing the office.

"I don't agree with your fiancée on most things, but on this one we are in agreement."

"Dad, I have a lead on an office in Glenview. A friend of Cindy's dad is retiring. It will take some time, which is good, because I can't just up and leave my patients."

He shook his head as he headed for his favorite brown La-Z Boy chair. Then he stopped and looked up. "What if I go to work with you as a kind of bodyguard until you're ready to close up?"

"Dad, I'm a big boy now. Also, the area is safer than it's ever been. There are police all over the place, and I already have a bodyguard. Nobody is going to bother me when Tyrone is around."

Actually, I knew my dad was right. I was just trying to finish up some cases and was waiting until something came of the office in Glenview.

Also, I've never been a quitter, and it was hard for me to just give up. So early Monday morning, I was back at my office on Madison and Halsted Street.

Monday, Tuesday, Wednesday, and no Darlene. Worried about her, I did a very dumb thing. I got in my car and drove over to Warren and Artesian. This neighborhood was different from Madison and Halsted. There were the same empty liquor bottles, boarded-up buildings, graffiti on the archways, and garbage in the gutters, but the streets were filled with young, tough, hard-eyed black youths, not burned-out, hollow-eyed old bums. I was apprehensive and fearful.

At 2415 W. Warren, Darlene's address, I stopped the car and kept a wary eye on the young men wearing gangland jackets who were eyeing me, in preparation to spring after the young white male who was invading their turf. I quickly walked up the worn-down, broken--windowed, red brick tenement building and knocked on apartment 216.

A very tired-looking black woman answered the door. Three or more barefoot little kids surrounded her, and a cigarette hung from her lip. A dog barked, something one didn't hear on Skid Row.

"What you want?"

I told her that I was the dentist Darlene worked for and I was looking for her.

"She's a good girl," the woman kept repeating.

"Where is she?" I asked.

"I don't know. Please don't make her lose her job. She my oldest."

"Is she with Tyrone?" I asked.

"He's no good. She a good girl." Her eyes were pleading with me to understand. Before she closed the door, my eye caught sight of a large boom box similar to one Tyrone carried around.

Carefully maneuvering the broken and garbage-laden steps, I made it out of the building, and back to my car. It was still intact. I guessed my VW was too old and too much of a wreck to be toyed with. As I walked around to the driver's side, a black Lincoln pulled up next to my car, blocking me from entering. A darkened window from the back passenger side lowered, and a round brown head with small, beady eyes looked me in the face.

"Doc, what you doing on Warren Street?'

"Looking for Darlene, my office girl."

A devilish grin formed on his face. "Get out of here. Stay in your territory. It's much safer."

I thought to myself, *Skid Row is safe?* To the man in the car I nodded, and got into my car, as Kohl, an ex-football player, the driver of the Lincoln, eased the car back. I had been given an order by Duke Wilson, the neighborhood numbers boss. Driving away, I wondered if Wilson had anything to do with the murders.

WONDERING WHETHER DARLENE WOULD SHOW up, the following morning I went to my office earlier than usual. As I exited my car and walked toward my building, the comfortable feeling I had attained this last year was exchanged by an eerie sense of danger. Skid Row was quite different since the killings. The streets were quiet and almost abandoned, and the vacant, boarded-up corner drugstore didn't help.

I became alarmed when my office door opened without a key. Stepping into the dark waiting room, I was suddenly grabbed from behind and a knife was stuck up against my neck. Closing the door to the office, my attacker directed me to the operatory. I didn't need to guess who it was.

"Tyrone, what are you doing in my office?" I asked in the most normal tone I could conjure up.

"Doc, I need your help." He released me and faced me. He looked desperate. Scared. He still held the knife close to my throat.

Trying to stay calm, I looked him in the eye. "Put down that knife and let's talk."

He lowered the knife but still kept it near me. "Spider, he double-crossed me. They picked him up, and he put them on my tail." Tyrone then reached in his pocket, pulled out a small bottle of something and took a drink. Junkies usually don't drink, so he was really going to be tough to deal with.

"Tyrone, I want to help you, but I can't think clearly with that knife in my side. I don't believe you killed the druggist."

"Don't matter, Doc. If those bastard white police think I did it they will fry me. Let's go, Doc; I need you to drive me out of this damn city."

I was gripped with fear as I tried to think of my next move. Getting in a car with this desperate junkie was suicide. Grabbing a cigarette from Darlene's desk, I offered it to him, in an effort to stall things. It was almost nine o'clock. Someone might come soon. Physically I was no match for this six-footer with a knife.

"I believe you didn't do it. Times are changing with the civil rights movement and Dr. King."

"Maybe for some nice, rich, famous black man, but not for us poor niggers."

"Let me get you a lawyer."

"Fuck you!" he yelled as he put the knife back up to my face.

"Don't hurt him, Tyrone."

Suddenly I realized my angel in the form of Darlene was standing in the doorway

"Tyrone, take his keys and his money. I will tie him up. I can drive while you stay out of sight."

He stood back, still holding the knife close to me. Darlene leaned in toward me and loosely tied me to the dental chair. She whispered, "Keep quiet and I won't let him hurt you."

"Put tape over his mouth. I don't need no screamin', now."

I let her tape my mouth, believing they would leave and I would be fine; that was until my eyes met hers. There was fear there.

TYRONE YANKED THE PHONE OUT of the wall, opened my medicine cabinet, and took out a bottle of codeine and took some pills. He looked at me with bloodshot eyes and walked to the door next to Darlene. She opened the door to leave, but he closed it.

I trembled as I heard bits and pieces of their heated conversation.

"No, Tyrone, I won't let you!"

"Shut your trap. We do it my way."

"Your way got us into this mess," Darlene said.

"I owed the money for my stuff. It was me or them."

"What about Spider?" Darlene asked.

"Spider, don't say his name. That mother-fucker, he double-crossed me."

I heard the door open and then slam closed. I cringed as I heard a howl come from Darlene. My back was facing them, so I didn't see what was happening, but when I heard Tyrone's footsteps coming toward me I felt a scream racing through my body toward my mouth, but I had no mouth! It was taped shut!

Just as a knifed hand came by my throat, a small hand covered in blood stopped it. Tyrone lowered the knife and looked into my horrified face, "You lucky, man, that girl really likes you."

He then turned around, grabbed Darlene, and pulled her through the office door.

Never had I been so frightened, never had I been so close to death. I knew I should hurry in my efforts to untie myself, but my body wouldn't respond. It took me at least ten minutes before I was even able to try. My mind kept going back to Miranda's comment a few months ago, *Baby, you still wet behind the ears.*

I untied myself, painfully removed the tape, took a deep breath, trying to slow down my heartbeat, stood up, and tried to get my trembling hands and feet to move. There was no phone and no one in the building, so I moved to the window to make sure my car was gone. Still shaking, and not sure Tyrone and Darlene had really left the building, I grabbed a pair of scissors and a dental instrument, and slowly moved out of the office, down the stairs, and into the pawn shop.

"Leo, help," I screamed as I collapsed on his swivel desk chair.

After hearing my story, he gave me a drink and called the police station.

I waited in the pawn shop for Detective Scarianno.

When he arrived he was accompanied by at least three men from the police department. They went upstairs to comb my office for evidence, while the detective sat down next to me.

He lit his cigarette and said, "Okay, Doc, sit back, relax, and tell me about your ordeal."

I took a drink of my coffee, and slowly related how Tyrone had almost killed me.

Scarianno took out a pad and pencil and asked for my car's description and license plate number, and a description of Tyrone and Darlene. He then walked over to the wall phone and called for a three-state alert for the car and the suspects.

Tired and wiped out, I asked him if I could call my dad and go home.

He answered, "I would like you to come down to the station and give us a written statement."

"Why?" I asked.

"We may consider you an accomplice to the crime."

"What?" both Leo and I asked.

One of the policemen came in. "Tony, you better read him his rights."

With that statement, I picked up the phone and called my dad. He met me at the police station with a lawyer, who arranged for me to go home, since there was no evidence to hold me or link me to the crime.

My mom wanted me to go to a doctor, but I just crashed for the next ten hours, only getting up to talk to Cindy. Two days later they found

Darlene and Tyrone stranded near the Indiana border. She was bruised badly, but all right. Tyrone was stoned. My old VW had blown a rod, and they were huddled in the car. Bad choice of a getaway car.

Darlene and Tyrone were locked up in county jail, awaiting trial. The newspapers declared the murders solved, and I never heard again from Detective Scarianno, so I assumed Tyrone confessed to committing the murders on his own.

I couldn't get Darlene out of my mind. She had tried so hard to do her job well, and she did save my life. I feared that being a black girl from the ghettos she would go down with Tyrone, so I called my lawyer, Don Jordan. On a Monday morning I met him at county jail, where we were directed to a small, windowless visitor's room, reserved for lawyers and their client.

Upon entering the room, we were surprised to see that Darlene's eye was still black and blue from Tyrone's beating, and her hand was bandaged from the knife wound. Jordan looked at me and whispered, "That will help her case," as he nodded toward her wrapped hand.

Darlene's surprised expression quickly melted into tears. "Oh, Doctor Greenberg," she sobbed, "I'm so sorry. I never wanted to hurt you, but Tyrone was stoned and crazy." She turned away from me and buried her head in her hands.

I put my hand on her head. "Darlene, you saved my life, and now I want to help you. This is Mr. Jordan. He's my lawyer."

Jordan motioned for me to wait outside. While sitting outside of the jail, I was approached by a black priest who held out his hand to me. "Son, I just heard what you done for Miss Darlene. Her mother told me you were a good man. Jesus will reward you."

EVEN THOUGH THINGS EASED ON the street, I was wiped out over my ordeal with Tyrone, so I caved in to my parents and fiancée and agreed to close the office and temporarily work for a friend on the north side.

On a Friday morning in late April my dad and I climbed into his old truck and headed to Madison and Halsted to close down my office. Turning toward my dad, I said, "You know, Dad, I feel sorry for Tyrone. It's hard to believe he killed both men. Abe was good to him, giving him merchandise and cigarettes on credit. I always thought he was all talk, and his friend Spider was the violent one."

"Mel, are you crazy. That dope addict almost killed you."

"You're right."

"Do you think he'll have a trial or they will just jail him for life?"

"In the old days they would just finish him off in county jail, but with today's civil rights he will go to trial."

"Dad, a lot of the people in the neighborhood think somebody, like the politicians or gang leaders, hired Tyrone."

We turned off the expressway on Madison Street, where we were stopped by several police cars. As we waited to go by, to our surprise a handcuffed Dr. Max Roy was being led out of his medical building and put into one of the police cars.

I quickly got out of the car and asked the people on the street, "What did Roy do?"

"Don't know." I smiled at the familiar answer to anything asked on Skid Row.

I had to wait until the morning to find out. The *Chicago Tribune* had a headline on the front page, "Double Murder on Skid Row Has A New Twist."

# CHAPTER 13

THE STORY THE CHICAGO PAPERS carried on the front page sounded like fiction to anyone but an inhabitant of Madison Street. A young black man named Tyrone Wilson had been arrested for the murder of Abe Meyer and Dave Miller. When caught and interrogated, he confessed that the dentist, Dr. Max Roy, had paid him to kill the druggists. Tyrone took a plea bargain—life in prison in exchange for testifying against Dr. Roy.

It took months before Dr. Max Roy went to trial. Meanwhile, my lawyer, Don Jordan, was able to get Darlene off on probation. I was even able to obtain a job for her with a black dentist who practiced in Hyde Park.

Against Cindy's and my dad's advice, I traveled to the courthouse in downtown Chicago and joined Leo for Roy's trial. Due to work, I had to miss the first day with the opening statements.

After entering the court room, Leo and I sat about four rows back. The first few rows were crammed with reporters. The next rows were reserved for family, but they were empty. I guess Roy didn't have any family interested enough to show up, Abe's family wasn't around, Tyrone's mom was a prostitute and junkie, and his dad was unknown so they were not there. Darlene was sitting in the very last row of the courthouse, and I think Dave's wife was back there also. I wasn't sure. Looking at her, I felt ashamed. I hardly knew Dave, and therefore I really didn't pay proper respect to his family.

I moved my gaze back to the front of the courtroom just in time to see Alderman Johnson, plus two other men sit down a few rows in front of us. I nudged Leo. The lighting in the old court building was dark, so I had trouble seeing who they were.

"All rise," the bailiff said as Judge Jerome Silento entered the room. I was surprised to see a short, thin young man, somewhere in his late thirties or early forties, take the bench. He took his seat at the bench, and in a clear, deep voice, he asked the two attorneys if they were ready to start the trial. .

Both attorneys approached the bench. The prosecutor, Mike Quinlin, tall, slim dark haired, was known for his wit and skill. Roy's attorney, Maxwell Broombaum, was short, heavy, and sporting a curled mustache that he constantly touched.

A handcuffed Tyrone was led into the courtroom. As the bailiff removed his cuffs and ordered him to sit down, his muscular six-foot-three body seemed to shrink and pull in. He no longer looked like a tough, confident gang member. He resembled a frightened, caged cat. His state-appointed lawyer did a smart thing with his plea bargain. It was probably the state-appointed attorney's idea. Quinlin knew he wouldn't get much publicity trying a young black junkie for murder, but a white doctor hiring a hit man to kill two white pharmacists would definitely put him in the spotlight.

The clerk called for the jurors to enter, and my gaze then turned toward them. Out of a pool of forty, the required twelve entered the courtroom and took their seats in the jury box. The alternates sat nearby. They seemed to be a pretty diverse group—white, black, Asian, eight men and four women. Most were dressed in business attire, suits and dresses. One girl, probably in her late twenties, was in hippie attire, blue jeans, and beads.

The judge directed the prosecutor to begin.

The prosecutor's first witness was a man who had known Dr. Max Roy for years. After being sworn in, Quinlin just asked his witness two questions.

"Mr. Valencio, did you know Dr. Max Roy when he was a wrestler?"

"Yes, he wrestled for years before and after becoming a doctor."

"In your relationship with Dr. Max Roy, over the last thirty years, would you say he has a violent temper?"

"I have seen him scream and curse, and throw—"

Broombaum stood up, and quickly called, objection, "This is opinion, not fact."

Quinlin smiled, "No further questions." He had established that Dr. Roy had a rough side to his character.

I looked at Dr. Roy and thought to myself, *He is really staying calm, and acting disinterested.* I was surprised when Roy's lawyer didn't cross examine Valencio.

The prosecutor then called his next witness, "Tyrone Wilson."

Tyrone, dressed in a neat tan shirt, brown pants, and cropped hair, looked taut and frightened.

The prosecuting attorney, Mike Quinlin, started his questioning.

"Please state your name."

"Tyrone."

The judge looked down. "Your full name."

Tyrone looked at his lawyer nervously.

Quinlin said, "The judge wants your first and last name."

"Tyrone Wilson."

"Your age?"

"Eighteen."

"Your address?"

I was surprised when Tyrone gave Darlene's address as his. He relaxed some now that his answers were right.

Quinlin turned from Tyrone to Dr. Max Roy. Pointing his finger in Dr. Roy's direction, he asked Tyrone, "Do you know the defendant?"

Tyrone mumbled a yes. The judge turned toward him, "Louder, please."

His eyes opened wide as he looked at the judge. "Yes, sir."

"Objection," Broombaum said. "His answer is not clear."

Quinlin leaned in toward Tyrone and said something.

Tyrone answered, "Yes, sir, I knows Dr. Roy."

"Did you work for him?"

"Sure, by the doc's office."

"What doctor?"

"Doc Greenberg." Tyrone turned and looked straight at me, and I shrunk down into my seat, refusing to make eye contact with him.

"Did Dr. Max Roy tell you that he wanted the pharmacists killed?"

Tyrone looked around the room like a caged animal hoping to flee before answering.

Roy's eyes were glued on him.

"Dr. Roy, he told me Doc Abe burned down his office so he was gonna get that bastard killed."

Roy jumped up with, "He's a God-damn liar."

"Sit down and stay quiet," the judge ordered Roy. Then he turned to Quinlin, "Before proceeding, will you inform your client that profanity is not allowed in my courtroom?"

The prosecutor approached Tyrone and quietly said something to him before proceeding with the questioning. *Lots of luck,* I thought.

Quinlin continued, "Did the defendant, Dr. Max Roy, ask you to kill Abe Meyers?"

"Yeah me or somebody I know."

By this time the courtroom was abuzz with gasps, and Roy's attorney was having a hard time holding him down. Dr. Roy leaped out of his seat and headed toward Tyrone.

He pointed his finger in Tyrone's direction, and in an outburst he yelled, "That stupid young punk overheard me ranting and raving about Abe. I said something in jest about wanting Abe dead, and he believed me." He was restrained by the court guards.

There was rumbling in the courtroom. I loved the grin on the prosecutor's face. He was being handed a good part of his case.

I watched Max Roy's attorney turn white as the judge hit the gavel, asking for order in the courtroom. A recess was requested.

Leo and I joined the reporters at the coffee machine. One of the reporters made an interesting comment. "It's a criminal trial, so Quinlin must get a unanimous guilty verdict. So far it's the word of a junkie who admitted to pulling the trigger against a doctor."

Another said, "I thought this would be dull. It just started, and already that lawyer, Broombaum, and Roy are putting on a show."

"Quinlin can go home, that Roy is going to bury himself," the reporter from the *Daily News* announced. "By the way, I saw Royko slip in. His column should be good tomorrow."

The reporter from the *Chicago Tribune* said, "Quinlin must have other witnesses. I know they had that kid that ratted on Tyrone, but they couldn't hold him, and now he disappeared."

Leo and I looked at each other while we mouthed the name Spider. We continued to eavesdrop, while standing by the door, sipping our coffee.

"In murder cases they usually have a family member as a witness."

*Hm,* I thought, *maybe that's why we don't see any of Abe's family in the courtroom.*

AFTER A FIFTEEN-MINUTE RECESS THE court room was opened and everyone piled back in. The judge directed the prosecutor to continue with his questioning of the witness. Roy was sitting very quietly, staring down at the floor.

Quinlin turned to the jury as he continued with his questioning. "Did Dr. Roy give you the gun?"

"No, Spider did."

"Is Spider your friend?"

"Friend. That double crossing …"

Quinlin cut Tyrone off. "Forget that question. Did you know the gun was stolen from the drugstore?"

"Yeah," Tyrone answered as he looked down at the floor.

"Were you contracted to kill both Dave Miller and Abe Meyer?"

"No, just Doc Meyer." Tyrone squirmed before putting his head down and mumbled, "I really liked him, but I owed the money for my junk. It was me or him."

From the back of the room Dave's widow stood up and yelled out, "Then why did you kill my husband?"

All eyes turned to the back of the courtroom, where a clerk was gently escorting Dave's crying wife out of the room.

Tyrone looked at the back of the room. "I'm sorry lady," Tyrone explained. "I got scared. I never killed nobody before. When he come out I thought he was the right one."

Dr. Roy screamed, "Liar," while his attorney was yelling, "Objection. The witness is responding to a question that was never asked by the prosecutor."

The judge was hitting the gavel while saying, "Order in the court! Broombaum, control your client. Objection sustained. Quinlin, continue your questioning." He leaned back in his seat with a sigh.

"What happened when you went to collect your money?'

"Doc Roy, he just be yelling, 'You dumb nigger, you killed the wrong man.' And he chased me with his big old nightstick."

Again, Max got up screaming, "You goddamn liar."

The judge looked at Dr. Roy. "We will take a fifteen-minute break. Clear the courtroom. Mr. Broombaum, please come up to the bench."

Judge Silento looked at Dr. Roy while addressing his lawyer. "Your client will be held in contempt of court if he continues with his outbursts."

The reporters hurried out of the courtroom to the phones. Leo and I went back to the coffee machines.

Quinlin emerged, smiling triumphantly. It had been rumored that he planned to use this trial to help him run for state attorney.

When the trial resumed, Max Roy was sitting very quietly, and Tyrone was shifting nervously in the witness box as the questioning continued.

"Did you collect your money after you shot Abe Meyer?"

"Spider come with me."

"Did Dr. Roy pay you?"

"Yeah, he gimme a check for three thousand dollars."

The prosecutor showed Tyrone and then the judge a cancelled check from Dr. Max Roy for three thousand dollars.

The courtroom was rumbling with surprise. Who would give someone a check for a hit, and where would a punk black kid cash it? Leo and I had learned from Darlene that Tyrone never saw the money. After Tyrone signed the check, Spider took it, allegedly to pay off Tyrone's drug debts.

Dr. Roy jumped up and headed for Tyrone, while screaming, "You goddamn liar, liar, liar."

While being subdued he collapsed on the floor, gasping for breath.

Pandemonium overtook the courtroom, with people rushing everywhere and cameras flashing, before the courtroom was finally cleared, and the doors closed.

We waited outside while an ambulance pulled up. Dr. Max Roy was rushed to the hospital, and court was adjourned until further notice. The papers kept a vigil by the hospital, reporting every day on Dr. Roy's condition. The case had taken bigger proportion now. I was even called by the *Chicago Tribune* for an interview.

Dr. Roy lingered in a critical stage for three weeks before his heart finally gave out, and the case was closed. By then it was old news, and it was reported on the third page of the papers. Other news had taken over the front page.

I guess we could say Tyrone lucked out with his plea-bargain for life in prison, but things didn't work out there for him either. Without his drugs and his buddies, he was just another scared young kid from the ghetto who ended up walking through life on the thorns instead of the petals. He only lasted behind bars in Joliet for nine months. According to the prison records, he was found stabbed to death in a bathroom stall.

NO ONE WANTED TO BUY the drugstore, so the building was torn down. Leo stayed in the area and we met a few times for lunch.

On our last meeting, I asked him, "What do you think really happened?"

"More to it," Clancy told me. "Abe had his hand in many pots, and no reporter was allowed near Dr. Roy when he was in the hospital."

"Roy did give Tyrone a check for three grand," I said.

"Somebody higher up used Tyrone and Dr. Roy to get rid of Abe. Chicago politics at work again."

I leaned back in my chair, trying to sort this out when Leo got up to leave.

"Keep in touch," he said.

We didn't. Our lives went in different directions. Cindy and I married and lived in the north suburbs. I caved in to safety and monetary rewards and opened a new office near my home. The only piece of equipment I took from my Madison Street office was the antique dental cabinet. When I left Madison Street, I was no longer that naïve, wet-behind-the-ears boy who opened his first dental office a year ago.

# CHAPTER 14

## 2012

As my plane prepared to land in Chicago, I stared out the airplane window at the ice-covered waters of Lake Michigan, the greenery peeking out through the two or three feet of snow, the cars racing along the super highways, the hundreds of high-rise buildings, and my beloved Soldier Field. *Yes,* I thought to myself, *after all this time Chicago still feels like home.*

Exiting the airplane, I slowly trudged down the corridor of O'Hare International Airport. The walk to the baggage retrieval center seemed to be a much longer distance than I remembered, but then again, lately I was lucky to even remember my name. I picked up my small, black, tattered suitcase, buttoned up my heavy coat, covered my gray head of hair with a matching gray wool hat, and slipped on my black leather gloves. Fifty years spent in Chicago taught me how brutal the weather could be in February, so I was prepared for this trip. When I stepped outside, I felt the cold wind howling by my face, and when I looked down at the ground, I saw a covering of beautiful white virgin snow. I considered picking up some of that lovely powdery stuff and making a snowball.

Shivering in the twenty-five degree temperature, I waited my turn at the cab stand. Finally, a yellow taxicab pulled up. The driver was barely old enough to be my grandchild. Worried that this young white kid might be afraid to travel where I was heading, I said, "I need to go to Madison and Halsted. I'll give you an extra tip if you'll take me to Skid Row."

He smiled. "Get in, old timer. From that remark, I can tell you've been away a while. Madison and Halsted is one of the nicest neighborhoods in the city. It is now called West Loop Gate. Where have you been?" he asked.

I warmed up to this nice young man, and true to people of my age, I started to tell him my life story.

"I'm a retired dentist living alone in Arizona. My wife Cindy passed away years ago. It's my first time back in Chicago in almost twenty years. I'm coming home for my granddaughter, Dr. Cheryl Lynn Greenberg's, dental office opening,"

Handing him a small business card with her name and address on it, like a true proud grandfather, I said, "If you need any dental work, she is the best. Good looker too. Cheryl comes from a long line of dentists. My son, a dentist too, went and moved west, to Arizona. That's where Cheryl grew up. In retirement, I followed him. When my granddaughter graduated from the University of Illinois at Chicago Dental School she decided to stay in Chicago, and my son and his wife moved back to the city to be near her. Go figure! Now I am the one living alone thousands of miles away."

"The address on the card is where you are going?" he asked.

"Yes," I answered.

"Must be warm in Arizona now. I've never been there."

"Around seventy during the day, but the nights can get down to the thirties. Desert, nothing like here."

The drive from the airport was all expressways until we turned off on Madison Street. I would have loved to drive down the outer drive like the old days before all these super highways. To me, Lake Michigan with its icy blue water beating against the rocks in winter and her beach-going bicyclists and walkers in the summer represented Chicago.

As the taxi approached Madison Street, my eyes opened wide in astonishment. I gazed upon clean, tree-lined streets, gardens, and high-rise apartment buildings with restaurants and stores one would only find on Chicago's exclusive North Michigan Avenue. I was gazing upon a thriving upper middle class neighborhood.

"We're here—eight-twenty West Madison Street. That will be twenty-five dollars."

"Thank you, young man," I said as I handed him thirty dollars and exited the taxicab.

I stood staring in awe at the building on the lot I once occupied. In front of me was a forty-story streamlined tower of dazzling glass and steel. On the first floor where a drugstore once stood was an enormous Dominick's with groceries, household items, clothes, pharmacy, and a Starbucks coffee shop. I went into the coffee shop, sat down at one of the small tables, and looked out the enormous glass window at men and women rushing down the street in their expensive clothes. The only familiar landmarks were the 90/94 expressway a block from Madison and Halsted, and of course the shopping carts. My eyes rested on a woman in a fur jacket and high-heeled suede boots standing outside of the store as a clerk loaded her groceries into her waiting BMW. No shopping carts loaded with junk were traveling down Halsted Street, and no old, shabby parked cars were on the street, only luxury cars like the passing Lexus that zoomed by in between the buses and taxicabs.

I looked at my watch and realized my family would be looking for me. I moved out of the Dominick's and into the ultra-modern elevator building. *Dr. Greenberg 2102,* the directory said. A nice young man held the elevator door open for me. I exited it as quickly as I could for an old man. I stopped a minute by the door to 2102, admiring the sign that said,

"Cheryl Greenberg, DDS." The first thing I saw as I entered the beautiful contemporary five-chair dental office was an elegant antique dental cabinet. On top of it sat three diplomas from the University of Illinois Dental School. They were made out to: Melvin Greenberg, DDS, class of 1966; Barry Greenberg DDS, class of 1989; and Cheryl Lynn Greenberg, DDS, class of 2012. Tears came to my eyes as I hugged my granddaughter.

LaVergne, TN USA
22 January 2010
170810LV00004B/8/P